bond Twenty Vagabond Twenty Vaga

D1335638

Other books by the same author:

Potter's Field (Vagabond Voices, 2014)
Redlegs (Vagabond Voices, 2012)
John Lennon. The Story of the Original Beatle (Argyll
Publishing, 2011)
An Anarchist's Story. The Life of Ethel MacDonald
(Birlinn, 2009)
Ascension Day (Headline Review, 1999)
Poor Angels and Other Stories (Polygon, 1995)

Aliyyah

Chris Dolan

with illustrations by

Mark Mechan

Vagabond Voices
Glasgow

Published on 29 May 2015 by
Vagabond Voices Publishing Ltd.
Glasgow
Scotland

ISBN: 978-1-908251-44-2

Printed and bound in Poland

Cover design by Mark Mechan

Typeset by Park Productions

The publisher acknowledges subsidy towards this publication from Creative Scotland

ALBA | CHRUTHACHAIL

For further information on Vagabond Voices, see the website:
www.vagabondvoices.co.uk

For My Family

The street looks different though I imagine nothing has actually changed. I've subtly refashioned my image of the old house every time I've thought of it. The stone is redder, the road broader, and the door older and heavier than I'd remembered.

The silence inside is new to me. A hush, like freshly settled dust. A taste in my mouth, of raw stillness.

There's the phone, and there's the hallstand. A single old coat where there used to be a ruckus of anoraks and scarves and duffels and hats and brollies. Photographs on the wall.

The kitchen's unrecognisable. Was it really so small and dull?

And there's the wireless. "Zenith". I say it before I see it. Etched in gold jagged lettering on mahogany. I knew the word long before I knew what it meant, or thought to ask. It didn't matter. The word was enough. Zenith.

The radio was ancient, and big, even for then. A magic cask. The dial is the only thing I've remembered accurately in the whole house. Helsinki. London. Moscow. A wheel behind glass, turning like the world on a secret axis. Paris. Berlin. Benghazi.

I turn it on, and it lights up; grumbles, as if rudely wakened. Then it makes the same old noises it always made. Whirrings and stutters and yelps. A kind of gargle, like emphysema in its lungs. Spin the dial and you sprint across the earth: an opera of barks and babble. I stall for a second on a woman's voice, like water running over pebbles. Istanbul.

I used to stand between it and the window, letting all those sounds and voices and distances pass through me. I amplified them. I was the whole world. Little me. Full to bursting with hurried messages, world leaders intoning, orchestras and pop singers, all possibilities. Women with voices like water on pebbles, soft hands henna'd.

And here I am again now. I close my eyes, try to pick up the past. Meg, Marco, Brenda, James. Fine-tune Mum soothing, hard hands hugging. Her distant voice, like me not quite on the station.

ALIYKAH

Tale of the Soldier and the Old Man

O nce Haldane woke everything was white. White ceiling, white walls, a white door open just enough to reveal a white corridor beyond. He moved his head and felt a murmur of pain somewhere. On the far wall the white was finally broken by an open window looking out on to a perfectly green tree with bright red buds. He dozed off and woke again to the same scene, several times over, until he was fully awake and strong enough to move his body. The same pain no matter which limb he moved. He pulled the white sheets back and saw that his left leg was bandaged from the ankle to the knee. He managed to sit up, and then stand without the pain becoming much worse. He hobbled towards the half-open door, and called out.

"Hello?"

Glancing back into the room he saw it contained only the bed he had been lying in and a chair, over which was a neatly draped uniform. Under the chair was a black box, about the size of a car battery, bent and battered. He turned and limped out into the long white narrow corridor.

After about ten steps it opened out into a landing, at the left-hand side of which another window framed another green and red tree waving in a perfectly blue sky. The steps down into the rest of the house looked steep.

"Excuse me?"

Leading with the bandaged leg and holding on to the banister he made his way slowly down. There were pictures on the wall, portraits, of men mostly. But he had to concentrate on the steps, each of them of different depth, like the ones in the old manse.

"Under the chair was a black box, about the size of a car battery, bent and battered."

The hall below had more portraits on the walls and a brightly patterned rug on the floor. There was a door to his left which must lead, he thought, out to the fruiting trees. A door behind the steps probably led to kitchens. In front of him were three more doors, one of which was open a crack and gave Haldane the impression of being occupied. On the flat he found he could walk more or less normally. He knocked and opened the door a little more.

"May I?"

The room was huge, several rugs or carpets, intricately patterned, covered less than half the floor. There were low tables made of carved wood, numerous chairs and divans, cushions of many colours on the furniture, all set on the floor's bright green tiles. On a table at the far end sat a samovar and two glasses, and at the window stood a small figure staring out into the sun and a garden.

"Sir? I'm sorry but I…"

The man turned around. He seemed to Haldane, perhaps because he was at the other end of such a vast room, tiny. Dressed in a long white robe, a light brown waistcoat over it, and an embroidered hat, the little man smiled and held both his hands in the air. Behind his little groomed beard his smile was welcoming. Haldane thought it the most perfectly uncomplicated smile he had ever seen.

"Captain Haldane! What a wonderful surprise. And you came all the way down yourself?"

"Sorry. Yes. I called but…"

"Forgive me, my friend. I was listening for you but unfortunately my listening is not as reliable as once it was. Come in, come in. Sit. Here, let me help you."

"I'll manage."

But the little man was already scurrying towards him, around chests and dressers and cushions. He took a hold of Haldane's arm and led him gently, as if the younger and taller man were the older and frailer, towards the table

5

with the samovar. He sat him down on a chair then sat himself at the other side on a large upholstered cushion.

"Tea?"

Seated now, Haldane took in the room around him. On the walls hung tapestries woven with rich blues and reds with gold threads gleaming. There were thick rugs on the floor and smaller ones on top of the carpets. The silver samovar in front of him was one of many. The cup and saucer seemingly waiting for him were elegantly painted china.

"Cardamom tea. It's all you've been drinking since you arrived."

Stained-glass lanterns and giant urns etched with Cyrillic script sat on the floor and on marble cabinets with filigree woodwork doors. Above, candelabras hung from the painted wooden ceiling.

"Drinking?"

"Well," the old man giggled, "I administered it to you. I have great faith in cardamom tea!"

Haldane reckoned that every colour known to man could be found in this room. There were four double windows on the left-hand wall, each of them open, letting in the cool breeze and the scent of fruit and blossom that mingled now, as he took the cup to his lips, with the spice of the cold tea.

"Since I arrived. … I'm afraid I don't remember exactly how…"

"Yes, of course. You have plenty of questions. Plenty of questions!" The old man laughed merrily at the idea. "And all of them shall be answered. You have nothing to worry you. Nothing at all. All you must do, Captain Haldane my friend, is recuperate. Get back your strength. Cardamom!" And the old man drank deeply.

Haldane felt that he did indeed recognise the taste of the tea though he had no memory of ever having had it before.

"Are there others here?"

"Others? Ah, you mean other soldiers. Like you. No no. Not at all. Just us."

"You and I? I'm sorry I don't know your name."

"Duban. My name is Duban, Captain Haldane. Pleased to meet you…" and again he giggled, "now that you are awake."

"Please, call me Thomas."

"May I? Thank you, Thomas."

"So, only you and I?"

"And Ma'ahaba. You will meet her in due course."

"Ma'ahaba? Did she put on these bandages?"

"Not at all, not at all. All my own work."

"You're a doctor, Duban?"

"Alas no. But I am old and have learned one or two tricks along the way. I do not think you are too badly hurt," Duban laughed gaily. "At least not beyond repair. And now that you have made your way down here and are sitting comfortably drinking cardamom tea, I am altogether more convinced you will make a full and speedy recovery. But my advice is – the counsel of an old man, not a physician – rest! Peace breeds, strife consumes. Not too many questions. Till morning. Do not tax yourself, Thomas. I shall make you a little light supper, while you sit perhaps for a few moments in the outside in the shade." He opened one of the French windows. "Some air, a simple dish of rice and lemon and cilantro, and you will be ready to face the world in the morning."

Duban smiled beatifically, his dark eyes glittering as he bustled towards the door. "Enjoy the garden. It is quite lovely at this hour."

"Excuse me? Sir? Where am I?" But Duban was already at the far side of the vast room and didn't hear him.

Haldane would have called it an orchard rather than a garden, and one that looked as though it had not been properly tended for a few years. But that only added to its beauty. Overgrown paths curling between trees heavy with foliage and fruit he couldn't name, a little burn – or perhaps some kind of man-made irrigation canal – wild flowers rocking in the breeze, all combined to give the scene a picture-book effect. He noticed for the first time a slight blurring in his peripheral vision which only added to the fabricated effect of the orchard. The dull ache persisted and he wondered now if it wasn't coming more from his neck rather than his leg. But Duban was right. Sitting outside in the dappled afternoon sun relaxed him. Finding out where he was and how he got there could wait.

He woke again, this time facing the window and the tree. His hair was damp with sweat but the breeze from the window made the room fresh. He remembered waking in the middle of the night, after a nightmare, though he had no idea now what it was about. Nor could he piece together the events that had brought him here. He could bring to mind the army base camp, but only vaguely. If he concentrated, he was sure, he would remember everything, but he didn't have the energy, or the desire, to do so now. This place brought back memories of another place, further back in time. His home, his childhood garden.

He got up and thought that the pain had eased a little since yesterday. He realised that when he had gone downstairs before – yesterday? – and met Duban he had been wearing only a gown, longer and of thicker cotton than you would get in a hospital back home. He decided he should put on his uniform. A slower process than he'd hoped. Not so much the pain, rather that his limbs seemed to move slowly. He managed his trousers and shirt, and decided that boots and jacket would be too warm. He couldn't see socks anywhere. He did see the box under the chair and recognised it now as a radio. Battered and scuffed, wires hanging loose and the back falling off. He knew nothing about radios. He turned the on-off switch but the thing was dead.

Downstairs, the big room with all the tables and divans and samovars was empty. He called out for Duban but there was no reply. He wondered if the old man could only lip-read, that he was actually deaf. There was a jug of cool water and glasses on the table where he had first sat yesterday, so he poured himself a glass, drank it down, and took a refill outside to the orchard.

In the morning sun the trees and the little gushing canal seemed in better order. He walked along one of the paths that coiled round the trees, stepped off into the grass and wild flowers, the fresh dew pleasant on his bare feet. He recognised a fig tree, and one he thought might be mulberry. Over there, walnut perhaps. And peach. A perfectly red, round fruit like a little apple. Then some cherry trees – just like in the manse garden. The orchard seemed to go on forever, until he spotted a line of tall palms and reckoned that must be the boundary. Getting closer, he noticed that behind the palms was a wall. A pale stone, almost pink in the morning light. As he approached it he realised it was extremely high, almost as tall as the palm trees. Craning his neck he saw barbed wire across the top. Haldane turned and walked back towards the house.

He sat on the bench at the French window and sipped his water. He mustn't dally too much. He was a soldier. Of some sort. He should find out exactly what his position was. Casualty, certainly. Prisoner perhaps? He hadn't felt like one until he saw the wire. He would find Duban and sort out what's what here. He laid his head back against the cool stone of the house and glimpsed, in the centre of the orchard, someone sitting. A woman, to his right, in a part of the garden he hadn't investigated yet. The trees there looked smaller, pruned and cared for. She was sitting, almost lying back, on a chair in a clearing where the sun shone uninterrupted by branches. Her hair tumbled

9

in black tresses almost touching the grass. Duban had mentioned a woman lived in the house. Haldane felt he should introduce himself, but she seemed so at peace that his presence even at a distance seemed an intrusion. As he stood up, still undecided whether to retreat indoors or announce himself somehow, the woman – Ma'ahaba? – stirred in her chair. She hitched her skirt up over her knees, to let the sun fall on her legs. Haldane stood still. He had expected the woman Duban spoke of to be a nurse. This woman wasn't dressed as one. Perhaps it was her day off. Or perhaps she was the lady of the house. No doubt he would meet her later. As he walked barefoot back to the French window, he felt that she had noticed him and was watching him but, turning his head, she was still sunbathing sleepily.

"Good morning, good morning, Captain Haldane!" Duban clapped his hands, standing just inside the glass door of the big room. "You are looking well and I think not limping so much?"

"I think you're right, Duban. I feel rested."

"Come in, sit down. I have breakfast for you. And now is the time to have all your questions answered."

They sat across the table from one another as they had done before. There was a samovar of cool cardamom tea and a plate readied for the soldier with flatbread, tomatoes, pomegranate seeds. Beside them a little glass jug of olive oil and a ramekin dish with a mix of dried herbs and spices.

"You shall eat. I shall speak." Duban looked up to the ceiling as if searching for inspiration while Haldane ate half a tomato, cool in his mouth.

"You have been here several days. You were brought here by friends of this family. You are a very lucky man. First to have survived the crash, and second to be found by our ally. You come to us, Thomas, like the proverbial babe – and proof that a man only possesses whatever will not be lost in a shipwreck! Ha. Except in your case of course, it was an aircraft." He paused and turned serious again. "You see, Thomas, you are among friends, but behind enemy lines. Were the insurgents to find you here…"

The herbs, Haldane thought, were only recently dried. They tasted fresh, pungent, and together with the oil and tomato almost an assault on the senses.

"Your base is over fifty miles from here. Beyond the border. Your regiment, I imagine, will have classified you as missing in action – MIA?" Duban seemed delighted by knowing the appropriate acronym. "But perhaps they believe you dead. Eventually we will be able to get word to them but that might take some time. The longer you stay here, the more dangerous for us all."

Haldane listened as he ate, but felt like a man hearing the story of some stranger. There were things Duban said that he recognised and others that made no sense to him. The old man beamed, his little angelic eyes sparkling:

"You are recuperating well – even better than I had hoped! I think you are a strong and healthy young chap. And steadfast. You will make a full recovery, no doubt about it. Within a few days, God willing, you will be able to leave us. But of course you cannot simply walk out the gates. You will need to be collected by your regiment – that in itself is a perilous enough venture. Our best bet, my friend – I have tried to think this through while you slept – is the radio. The ally who found you – a cousin of this family – had the presence of mind to find the radio in the helicopter and bring it with him. I think perhaps it is broken?"

"Looks like it."

"But you can make it work again?"

"I'm sorry, but I know nothing about radios."

"Oh, dear. I had hoped… Well then we shall just have to study the contraption and see if we cannot use our combined wits to identify what is wrong with it and repair it. It shall be our pastime!"

"We can try, I suppose. Duban, sorry but I don't remember… a crash? Helicopter crash?"

"I think this is to be expected. After trauma, short-term memory loss. I looked in some books. My collection is quite old but there is wisdom I think in old books. Do not worry. Everything shall fall back into place. All you need is more cardamom tea!" Duban laughed uproariously.

"My injuries. You bandaged my leg…"

"Yes, you were bloodied when you arrived. But miraculously once I washed you down I found only a bad gash in your leg. We have penicillin here. I mixed it with your tea and spoon-fed you the concoction as you slept."

"I think you saved my life."

"Not I, Thomas, no. You did. Youth, strength, pluck. That's it, pluck! You and God – He must have a special use for you! The man who found you, he said you weren't breathing as you lay on the ground. Only when he lifted your head did you begin again. And here, under my care, from time to time your breathing became very shallow and slow. You seemed to suffer headaches even whilst you were unconscious. When that happened I made the tea extra strong and mixed in a few peppery spices – it seemed to do the trick!"

"The man… your ally. Did he find anyone else?"

Duban looked directly at Haldane, his old eyes moist and soft. "I am afraid Thomas your comrades died in the crash."

"How many of them?"

"You remember nothing of it? Not even before leaving camp?"

"Sorry."

"Two others, I believe. Our man could not be sure."

A bitter sorrow came over Haldane. Who were these men? It was his duty to concentrate and remember them. Comrades who had perished while he had lived.

"I'll spend the rest of the morning making myself remember."

"Do not do that. Your memories will return, all in good time."

"I'm thinking the way my eyes are seeing. Everything a little blurred. Like when I was a boy and put on my father's glasses."

Duban clapped his hands. "You spoke about your father. As you lay sleeping."

"I did? What did I say?"

"Oh nothing that made much sense to me. Just murmurs."

"Did I speak of anything else?"

"The war, perhaps. War is a terrible thing, Thomas. Best not to recall it to the waking mind too soon. Wait until you are sufficiently strong."

"I saw the lady you mentioned. Outside."

"Ah. Yes. Good."

"We didn't speak. I mean, she didn't see me."

"Ma'ahaba is the wife of Deimos, my nephew. You will recall General Deimos when your memory returns. For the moment all you need know is that he is the head of one of the few families in this region in alliance with your army. Thus, you were saved."

"General Deimos is not here?"

"And has not been, my friend, for several years. Nor do we expect his return until this wretched war is over. Most of our kin too are out in the field or working with governments abroad. Though we are not as numerous as once we were, alas."

"The portraits in the hall – they're all of this family?"

"Military men for the most part. Yes."

"But you are not? A military man. Or maybe you once were?"

Duban smiled. "We each must find what is requested of us." Then he laughed. "There must be at least one warrior for peace."

Haldane did not go straight to his room after breakfast but, at Duban's suggestion, took another walk in the orchard. This time he set out with purpose, to discover the shape and dimensions of his temporary home. He found immediately, sticking to the side of the house, that it was much grander than he had realised. Until now he had only seen his upstairs room, the corridor and steps and the great chamber where he spoke with Duban. He had imagined that there were kitchens behind somewhere and of course rooms for Duban and Ma'ahaba. But behind that part of the house the building, or rather buildings, stretched deep into the gardens. The stonework looked older the further back he walked. New additions had been constructed, he reckoned, over decades, perhaps centuries. The soldier knew little of architecture, even less in this part of the world, so he had no way of dating the different styles of stone- and brickwork. At the centre the house extended up to a third storey, and above that a narrow tower of creamy stone with arched windows overlooked the entire construction.

Reaching what looked like the back of the house he kept walking. In this direction the gardens seemed never to end. At first there were more trees, few of which he could name. Apple, more cherry, lemon or lime. One ancient-looking specimen with astounding orangey-red flowers that looked as if it came from the tropics. Given what Duban had told him about the family, there must have been some time in the recent past when the family was grander, with servants and gardeners, and perhaps not so cut off from the world. Before the war. The little channels of irrigation curled off in all directions, their overgrown untidiness making them look like natural springs. Heading straight through the trees, protecting him from the sun above, he saw signs of other small buildings that had either disintegrated through time or had been knocked down.

He heard the birds before he saw them. A soft whistle

at first, then a tapping he knew must be a woodpecker. He glimpsed for a moment a green spark high up on one of the tallest trees, some kind of parrot. As he followed a little stream round a copse he came to a small, thick tree, alive with little white birds with black plumes. Scores of them chattering.

It took him some time to find the perimeter wall. Behind the barbed wire he saw great mountains in the distance. High and remote and craggy. He felt he recognised them. Perhaps he had been in helicopters there before the last one crashed and brought him here. Staring towards the peaks, he saw a large bird launch itself off the wall and headed out into the silent open space beyond. He thought perhaps it was some kind of falcon. He saw no sign of Ma'ahaba, except once he thought he caught movement out the corner of his eye. A flash of white. But his peripheral vision was still blurry and doubtless it was one of the little white birds, or a blossom swaying in the breeze.

In his room Duban had left some basic tools and two books. A 1950s history of wireless communication and an old children's guide to how radios work. Haldane doubted if either would be of much use, but he put the radio on the bed and flicked through the pages. There were diagrams, but of much earlier apparatuses. He managed to take the back off the radio. Certain wires and configurations bore a resemblance to the pictures in the books. He had no idea where to begin but he tinkered a little using the old screwdrivers and pliers Duban had left.

Tired, he lay out and allowed himself to doze off. But the sleepier he got the more he became aware of aches and pains. His leg throbbed, and still that general pain which now he felt most keenly in his shoulders and neck. His felt as if his head was being forced back, against a hard chair, yet he was lying on his bed. As he drifted towards sleep he dreamed, or perhaps remembered, being in a helicopter.

He was thrown around by its jerky movements and the engine made a terrific noise. A man sat in front of him, at the controls. He felt he knew the pilot, but with only his back in view he couldn't bring the man's face to mind, or his name. And there was another soldier behind him. They were all laughing. The man behind shouted over the noise and the pilot in front pointed down towards the ground. They all laughed more. Haldane strained to look out the window and saw below the mountains, and amid them the old house and orchard and just visible a woman lying, apparently naked, between the trees. Then the helicopter suddenly jolted violently, and he thought he heard a woman's voice call out to him.

"Thomas!" But when he managed to wake fully and make his way out the room it was Duban waiting for him at the foot of the stairs. Haldane descended haltingly and was about to enter the great room when the old man stopped him. "Tonight you are well enough to eat at a table. The captain's table, aha!"

He followed the old man out through a door behind the staircase and along a similar corridor to the one above, with more portraits, then into a narrower, older passageway with several doors at either side. They came to another little hallway, almost a replica of the one below his room but lit only from a skylight above. Duban opened a door.

"Before we go through. Look!"

Haldane stepped into the room. The library wasn't large but all four walls were stacked to the ceiling with books and manuscripts and papers. Down the middle of the chamber were more bookcases, some of them modern, basic metal frames, others antiques, rich dark woods. The books themselves, like the orchard, looked like they had once been perfectly ordered and stacked, probably catalogued, but could do now with tidying up and reorganising. Duban looked into the room with unconcealed devotion.

"There haven't been many new additions in recent years. But there are wonders here. So many years I have spent in this room and even I still discover books I never knew existed."

He closed the door gently as though it were the room of a sleeping child, then led Haldane across the hall into another room.

The soldier felt he had entered another country: a country he knew better. Down the centre of the room was a long table set about with twelve chairs. The kind of table his mother would have liked. What she would have called up to date. Highly polished with a reddish glow. The far end was set for three: napkins, glasses that looked like the Caithness glass his mother was also fond of, cutlery and white supermarket crockery, a bottle of red wine.

"Be seated Captain. Tonight dinner shall be served to you in a way befitting your rank."

From a second door into the room appeared Ma'ahaba, carrying a stainless steel hostess tray. She wore a mink-coloured lace top that showed her shoulders, and a skirt to below the knee. Her dark hair was combed now, thick and sleek, looping round her shoulder and down her neck and breast. Haldane thought her very beautiful.

"Captain Haldane. Forgive me for not introducing myself earlier. Duban tells me that I completely ignored you this morning. Sorry – I was dead to the world."

"Please. No problem. Nice to meet you."

She smiled and nodded but did not approach him. "Likewise."

"You look very charming tonight, Ma'ab," Duban said.

"Thank you. One must make an effort for guests. I don't often have the opportunity."

She placed the tray on the table, keeping her back straight and bending at the knee gracefully. "I imagine,"

"… there are wonders here. So many years I have spent in this room
and even I still discover books I never knew existed."

she said, "you might crave some traditional food. Roast beef is impossible in these conditions so I have made curry. Is that still a staple these days?"

"It is, yes."

She served both him and Duban; the best dressed person was serving the still barefoot soldier and the old man in his simple robe. Duban thanked her profusely. She crossed to another cabinet and took out a heavy earthen pitcher. "We don't have wine here either, but sometimes a little is smuggled in. This, the guerrillas tell me, is from Hanat. It has to be decanted hours before. But I find the lees make a good compost for my herb garden." She poured a glass for Haldane. "This is our last bottle."

"Then please don't use it for me."

Ma'ahaba spoke with perfect English enunciation and Haldane became conscious of his coarser Scots.

"What better excuse could there be, Captain?" She poured herself a glass, put down the pitcher and poured Duban a glass of rose-tinted water from a jug.

The curry tasted almost exactly as Haldane remembered it from restaurants back home and the wine, though it smarted a little in his mouth, gave him relief from his aches. They chatted over dinner like colleagues in a canteen. Haldane asked how ingredients that weren't to be found in the orchard were acquired and was told that allies of the family made deliveries of foodstuffs and other essentials whenever they could.

"The General organises regular supplies to be sent from the capital." The General being Deimos, Haldane concluded, Ma'ahaba's husband.

"Despite being so remote, we are blessed, and want for little," said Duban.

"The General," Ma'ahaba continued, "sends when he can preserved foods."

"Pickled beetroot, ginger jam, preserved lemon, myrtle berries," Duban explained eagerly. "Though we have here in the gardens pistachio, peaches of the Omani variety, Indian gooseberry –"

"Usmani quince, jasmine. And aloe wood and ambergris –"

"To sweeten the burning wax."

Only then, looking around him, did Haldane realise that there were no electric lights in the house. So far he had woken when it was light and fallen asleep before nightfall.

The subject of supplies and General Deimos's generosity exhausted, Haldane was interested to know about the woman of the house. What had brought her here and what was it like to live with only the old man as company. Ma'ahaba, her eyes glowing with the peppery wine they shared, spoke contentedly. "I miss spaghetti and ice cream. And champagne. Baked beans!"

"Ma'ahaba studied at Cambridge," Duban informed the soldier proudly.

"Only my master's. I was at Durham. History and politics before a master's in international relations. Much good it did me. I met the General here, home in the capital seeing my parents before embarking – or so I thought – on a diplomatic career."

And now Haldane noticed the faintest trace of an accent in her voice. As she told her story he had the opportunity to look at her more closely. Her brown eyes, groomed dark brows, the swell of her bosom. He tried to find clues in her conversation as to what age she might be. She had the confidence and the full figure of a woman some years older than him. The way she dressed he thought might be old-fashioned, though that could be due to availability of clothes in such a secluded place. But there was not a line on her face, her hair luxuriant, and her conversation and laughter almost girlish. Once or twice he thought she caught him staring at her. If she did, she didn't seem to mind.

"My family, unlike The General's, has a long association with England. I had a ball there. A ball!"

Duban became uneasy as Ma'ahaba poured a third glass for herself and reminisced about parties, swimming in the sea, public houses and nights out with her student friends. He began to clear away the dishes, interrupting her to ask where she wanted bowls and spice mills put, though he clearly knew the answers to these questions. Ma'ahaba seemed not hear or notice him, prolonging, Haldane thought, what must be a rare night of conversation, and with a stranger. For his part he could think of little to say, his memory still hazy and the wine adding, not unpleasantly, to his blurred thinking.

That night he experienced the dark for the first time. A lamp was burning in his room though he had no memory of Duban or Ma'ahaba leaving dinner to light it. Its vapour was fragrant, scented presumably with the ingredients they had told him of, and filled the room with a dark leafy glow. Not so bright to obscure the stars outside his open window, flaring in their millions as though straining to be free of the sky. He lay on the bed, cooling in the draft from the window and as he closed his eyes he heard the helicopter engine again and saw the face of the pilot. He remembered his name now. Michael. No memory of a surname, but definitely Michael. Sitting next to him, in helmet and uniform the second flight officer – until she turned round and he saw Ma'ahaba's face, a smile on her lips. But he was not fully asleep and knew her to be a dream. Wishful thinking, and he laughed. Perhaps a sign of his strength returning? In the glow of the room he thought he could still see her, in the doorway, looking in on him. She was a beautiful woman after all, and surely lonely, cooped up here with an elderly brother-in-law.

When sleep overtook him again he was with Michael, and the other officer who had been operating the radio. Sam? They were not in the 'copter now but in some kind of makeshift bar with bottles of cold beer and all three of them were talking and smiling. Haldane felt that if he concentrated enough he could make out their words. Michael was speaking, explaining something, but all Haldane could hear was a distant murmur.

When he woke the murmuring continued. He waited for it to fade like the rest of the dream, or the memory, but it persisted. As he lay there looking out the window, the branches of the fruit tree rippling blackly against the stars, the pilot's voice was still whispering in the distance. Except now it sounded more like a woman's voice. And still it didn't disappear. Until he was convinced he was actually hearing someone somewhere talking, downstairs perhaps, or closer and whispering. Whether Ma'ahaba's or Duban's voice he couldn't tell. The old man had a wafer-thin voice, highly pitched.

Haldane got out of bed and made his way, frowning at the pangs of pain, towards the corridor to see if he could hear any better. There could be no doubt, the voice was not a dream. A little stronger than before, and he thought it came from above him rather than from the room below. He remembered that there was a third floor, visible from outside in the orchard, but whether directly above him or not he wasn't sure. He had never seen any steps leading upwards. Reaching the little upper hall, he caught sight of the portrait that hung there and the face of the family ancestor seemed to censure him. He could see no light shining from the great chamber below. Whoever was talking, he decided, it was none of his business. His father would have told him that he was being meddlesome.

So he returned to lie in his bed and let the constant whispering lull him back to sleep. A rhythmic gentle pulsing that quietened the low growl of the helicopter engine.

In the morning, feeling freshened, he did not go down at once to breakfast but tried his hand again at the workings of the radio. It began to make a little sense to him: a certain pattern to its tiny plugs and sockets and connections. He carried it over to the window so he could inspect it in the light. He noticed for the first time that a section was bent and a little blackened, a missing metal plug here and there, one or two others loose. His eye was caught by something moving in the garden below him. Ma'ahaba, robed entirely in white, head to toe, which surprised him, strolling through the garden a few trees back from the house. He turned back to the radio. Concentration was good. Perhaps if Duban had some wire in the house he could devise makeshift replacements. But would a house without electricity have such a thing? And if there was no power was the entire enterprise a waste of time?

He was about to don his uniform when he noticed that alternative clothes had been left to him. A pair of loose trousers, a light full-sleeved shirt and a pair of simple leather slippers. Much more practical than his own heavy clothes. There was even a little scarf. He had noticed that both his hosts wore one round their neck, presumably to protect against the sun.

Haldane put on the trousers and shirt, but left the scarf. Walking downstairs he felt underdressed. He remembered a joke of his father's: "Disgraceful. I'm quite certain they were naked under their clothes." Now the soldier did feel naked, and a little vulnerable, under his new regalia.

Duban was nowhere to be seen. There was a jug of cool cardamom tea, on the table, slightly bitter but refreshing in the rising heat. If they could keep something cool perhaps there was some form of power, a generator maybe? He took his glass out into the garden and headed towards where he thought he had seen Ma'ahaba. But the orchard was confusing, disorienting. Turning back he could no longer see the house, despite its size. He enjoyed the game of finding his way back, his leg giving him less bother today. The challenge reminded him of childhood walks, his father getting distracted by some plant or other, or a butterfly, and leaving young Thomas behind. His father always turned up a moment or two later with some new marvel for the boy.

He soon spotted the house, from a different angle than he'd seen it before. There was the third storey he'd seen before, set higgledy-piggledy to one side as if it had once been the centre of another house whose lower sections had now vanished. And next to that, nearer his own room, which he recognised by the fruit tree reaching up to it, was yet another bit of construction, like an outcrop. An attic. Ma'ahaba's living quarters? If so he could easily have heard her voice which would explain last night's whispers.

"Tell me about the war."

"All wars are the same, Thomas." Duban sat on a low stool under the canopy of an ancient tree, like a man in a pew under a vaulted church roof. Haldane leaned against the tree trunk.

"One war leads to another and then another. War breeds war. The offspring bear a great resemblance to their parent."

"But what about this particular war, Duban?"

"No doubt distinguished by its unique weapons, the design of uniforms and medals and flags. Particular massacres, atrocities. It came out of the last war and will lead to the next."

Haldane smiled at the old man. "You think a lot, Duban. I didn't say tell me about war, but about the war. This war. I'm only trying to remember."

"Then I am of no use to you, my friend. They are all the same to me."

Haldane sat on the grass and kept his back against the tree. "Is war always evil? Doesn't it show nobility, courage?"

"Perhaps, perhaps it can. But to what end, I wonder?"

Haldane thought for a moment and asked: "If each war

stems from the last, then there must have been a First War? The daddy of them all."

"I think that is possible. A battle so long ago and in so distant a place that we cannot now comprehend who or what started it or what it was about. All we know is, it was never finally won or lost. As no war ever is."

"You sound like my father."

"By the tone of your voice, Thomas, that is a mixed blessing?"

"He was a good man. A minister."

Duban clapped his hands and laughed. "I thought so! It is your fate, Thomas, to be surrounded by clerics!"

"I suspected as much."

"For what reason, I wonder?! Because I am old and ugly and tedious! Because I tend towards sermonizing, as you have just witnessed, rather than conversation."

"No. For the way you tended me, and still do. And all the books."

"Your father had books too?"

"This whole place..." Haldane looked around, over towards the house half-hidden behind leaves and jewels of hanging fruits. "It's so foreign, mysterious. Nothing is like the way it was at home. Your books look different from his, smell different. I can't name most of the things I see here. And yet, it reminds me so strongly of the manse, its little garden."

"Ah, a house is a house, a room a room, a tree a tree. All things, underneath their little local differences, are the same."

But Haldane still stared at what he could see of the building. "That part of the house is higher than that one. But I haven't seen any stairs up."

"Constructed, as no doubt you have calculated, at different times, by men with different aspirations and ideas of home."

"But how does one get from the second floor to the third?"

"There is nothing up there. With only Ma'ahaba and I here, we need less than a quarter of the rooms."

"But I thought I heard… Doesn't Ma'ahaba have her apartments up there?"

Duban got up and took his stool. "Due I imagine, though I am no architect, to the particularities of the building, sound travels in odd ways. I too have noticed that." He began walking towards the house. "Tell me. The radio."

Haldane followed him. "Doing my best. Working in the dark I'm afraid. You have no access to electricity here?"

"Oh something can be arranged I'm sure. Even less than an architect I am no electrician. All that reading and I have learned nothing useful! But we can consult our allies here and General Deimos. They have worked wonders for us before."

As they came to the door that led directly into the large chamber, Haldane decided to walk a little longer alone.

Turning round to the back of the house he discovered it was, or at least had been at some time, the front. There was a portico flanked by grand colonnades. On its roof were what Haldane first thought were gargoyles. Coming closer he saw they were depictions of real people. More members of the family, like the painted portraits he had seen inside. They stared back sternly at him. There was a central entrance on a pediment, the doors themselves ancient-looking, distressed and splintered. Haldane looked for a handle but there was none to be seen. He put his shoulder against the wood but the doors remained rigidly shut.

Stepping back down from the porch he could see, through overgrown trees, the outline of an old path. He decided to see where it led. Fighting his way through branches and thorns he kept to its fading course.

Eventually the trees and shrubs and weeds thinned out and he was able to walk upright for a distance. At the end of it was a gate. Not the original he thought, approaching it. Heavy, hulking slabs of grey iron, factory made, with barbed wire on top and laced through the metal spokes. He looked through, beyond into the empty, dusty surrounding terrain. There seemed to be nothing between the house and the distant hazy mountains.

Having gone back to his room to collect the pliers and back to the gate Haldane now busied himself by the window trying to fix little slivers and shards of wire into the minuscule holes of the radio's motherboard. He cut his finger several times on both the barb and the pliers and sucked the blood away.

Working at something, even this, unsure of what he was doing or why, helped bring back memories. He still couldn't remember the pilot's second name but the other officer – a flight lieutenant – Samuel? No, something like that. And the fact that he himself wasn't a proper soldier. Not a fighting one. At least he had no memory of ever being in a battle. He had some other duty. And that realisation led his thoughts down a different path.

There had been a fight. A quarrel. One that he knew preyed on his mind before his memory had been dimmed by the crash. He recognised the feeling of regret, of something unfinished before anything of the dispute itself came to mind. But now it did, fraction by fraction. It had been with his father. A row. Haldane could picture him – only just, not seeing clearly his own father's features – sitting behind his books, looking despondent, close to tears. He could hear his own voice shouting. Not the actual words but the unmistakable tone of defiance and self-righteousness. And then he could make out a single phrase – though perhaps he was confusing it with this afternoon's discussion with Duban. "Is it not the mark of a man to fight?"

Then, somewhere in the garden, he heard Ma'ahaba singing. It sounded like some kind of lullaby, soothing, not too much variety in its melody or expression but soft and sweet and hypnotic. He strained his head out the window to see where she was but there was no sign of her. With the rhythm of the woodpecker and chatter of distant birds Ma'ahaba's voice sounded like the breeze, as though it were her song rustling the leaves in the orchard and not the breeze itself.

Dinner that night was in the same room as before, though it took Ma'ahaba some time to appear. Duban and Haldane talked about many things: the soldier's health, then the old man's – apparently excellent – the healing properties of certain foods and plants, and finally the war.

"No news is good news, is that not the expression, Thomas? When you were brought here I was told that the front had moved a good way away from us and that we are safe here for the time being."

"Will they let you know when we're not?"

"Excepting complications, yes. But we must plan for the worst, no? There is no need for panic, but the sooner we can get you to safety the better."

"I am putting you in danger."

"We will not be forgiven for harbouring an enemy. But if the opposing forces reach our gates then we are in big big trouble anyway." Duban squealed with laughter as if he had cracked a fine joke, and ate his spiced chickpeas with relish.

When Ma'ahaba came in she did so as if the three of them had eaten together for months like this. No longer dressed up she wore a long embroidered gown that Haldane thought could be either a housecoat or a dressing gown. She had tied her hair up, with pins and little clasps, leaving tendrils of hair around her neck. Her slippers were beaded leather and she shuffled in them rather than walked.

"What have you been doing today, Ma'ahaba?"

"You wonder, don't you? How do I spend my time in this

place in the middle of nowhere. Do not worry about me, Captain."

"Please. Thomas."

"Oh but how often do we have a captain among us! Your name – sorry, but I'm sure you agree – is a fairly common one. Captain has much more of a ring to it. Virile and brave and pleasingly ceremonial!" She laughed and sat back in her chair, crossing her legs. "I have plenty to do. I write. Letters. Lots of them. I tend to my herb garden and then I marinade fruits and spice vegetables, and preserve them in jars. And I read. Exercise. And walk. Make plans. The question is, what do *you* do all day, Captain Haldane?"

"I have to admit, compared to you…"

"Thomas is resting, Ma'ab. Under my strict orders!"

"He's a man of action, Duban. And one, I imagine, not used to being by himself."

"I'm sorry. Could I be of some use?"

"Do you feel the world has forgotten you? Thinks you are dead yet goes on about its business merrily."

"Our guest is recuperating, Ma'ahaba," Duban furrowed his brow, a little theatrically Haldane thought. "And we none of us know how severe his injuries are. And he is fixing his radio, aren't you, Thomas?"

"Life is what you make it, don't you think, Captain? We all know it's possible to be lonely in the crowd. You can live in the busiest part of New York or Buenos Aires and have nothing to do on a Saturday night. Long-married couples feel alone or pass the time actively despising one another. And who was it said the world is full of people who dread death yet are bored on Sunday afternoons."

"I heard you singing."

Duban filled Ma'ahaba's water glass then said, "She has a lovely voice." But Ma'ahaba made no comment.

Haldane was drinking only water yet felt woozier than when he had been drinking wine. He lost the thread of the conversation – if, indeed, there had been any – until he heard Duban say, "Of course you're right. The gardens tickle me. So many years surrounded by them, the same trees and channels and plants and birds, and yet I often think I have seen something new." Duban was talking to him, as though answering a question, though the soldier couldn't remember asking one.

"It has almost the opposite effect on me. It is completely new to me yet I sometimes feel as if I know it."

Duban gave his little high laugh. "Then perhaps what you heard was a memory, not something new at all."

"Your memory is returning," Ma'ahaba contributed, "but not in the way you expected."

"There we have it! Fruitless to look for something which is not there."

The old man said it with a note of finality, the question settled. Haldane couldn't quite say why, but his tone nettled him. "Forgive me, Duban. But didn't you say you were a priest? Then isn't that precisely what you do – look for what is not there?"

Duban did not seem put out in the least, but answered merrily. "Ah, but if I understand your meaning, then there is no need to look. I take it you mean Spirit, or the Divine. Then, my friend, it is most certainly there. Like salt in sauce. You would only notice it were it removed."

"Or wouldn't have missed it had it not been added in the first place?"

To which Ma'ahaba threw back her head and laughed. "Uncle, you have a feisty one here. You see? A warrior. The minute he senses battle…"

"And the mightiest warrior," Duban replied, "is he who conquers himself."

The helicopter plummeted throughout the night. He was seated behind the pilot who, when she turned, was Ma'ahaba, hauling at the lever and cyclic, exulting in the noise of the dive. She leaned forward and worked some control on the panel that opened the windshield and the rush of air deafened Haldane and thrust him backwards. Ma'ahaba stood up and yelled for him to do the same. "Hang on to me, Captain!" He managed to get to his feet, his leg aching in the cold. She reached behind her, found his arms, and pulled them round her waist like a pinion rider on a motorbike. She thrust the cyclic and the 'copter pulled sharply out of its dive, turned upwards, so that for a moment they were facing the sky, Haldane hanging on tight to her to stop himself falling over. She feathered the pitch of the rotor blades, straightening up and gaining speed.

Below, he could see lights and the silhouettes of hills. Hills that looked more like those of his home country than war-torn ridges and rocks. Ma'ahaba's hair billowed in the rush of air, her body soft and sumptuous under her air-man's uniform.

She spoke to him but he couldn't hear her words. Just a murmur, gently repeated, like a prayer.

He found the front of the house again, the porticoes with statues of the family ancestors, their eyes blank and dead. Although he had dreamed all night – waking at times ter-rified, at others calmed by images and memories of home and childhood – he felt stronger today. Turning the corner at the far end of the house, its walls here some kind of sandstone, crumbling to the touch, he came across a low wall. Leaning over he saw what must be Ma'ahaba's herb garden. Straight little rows of green shoots next to yellow leaves and miniature shrubs. At the far end there was a glass-paned door which might, he reckoned, lead to the woman's living quarters. There was no other way into the miniature terrace, other than clambering over the wall. Haldane was tempted but thought better of it. A single window was closer to this end of the patio.

Some of the plants had labels on them, written in a neat hand. Ajwain. Myrrh. Indian hemp. At the centre stood the only tree, or large shrub, heavy with pomegranates. Along the side, near the door, were pruners and spades, pots and a bucket, under a tap dripping water.

He had expected to see Ma'ahaba come out the door onto the patio but instead caught sight of her out in the orchard proper. She was dressed again all in white, a shawl or mantilla over her head. She appeared, between trees, for only a moment, but not so far away that she wouldn't have seen him, yet she ignored him completely. He called out to her but she didn't answer. Irritated, he sat on the wall for a moment, looking at where she had appeared, but she never emerged from the copse he had seen her enter. As he got up to go, round the back of the house this time, he saw in through the patio window, and there was Ma'ahaba sitting reading.

She couldn't possibly have had time to return to the house, certainly not without him seeing her. Also, she was not dressed in white, but in the embroidered gown, its threads gold and red, she had dined in before. The book lay on her lap and her gown was open at the neck and thigh. He was sure she knew he was there, looking in on her, but she never raised her eyes from the page.

"There is someone else in this house."

Duban busied himself setting a salad of seeds and nuts before Haldane. "In what sense, my friend?"

"In the ordinary sense, Duban. A woman. There must be."

"Are we not company enough for you that you wish more? It is a quiet life we lead."

"I saw her. Dressed in white. And I think it was her I heard singing, or talking, the other night."

"As I say, Thomas, the zephyrs in the trees, the birds. There are martens and marmots, sometimes a fox. We are never alone," Duban clapped his hands, "in God's great creation!"

"None of those things speak or sing, Duban."

"Haha! Do they not?"

"Nor wear white cloaks with hoods."

Duban looked at him and for the first time Haldane saw sadness, or some kind of solemnness, in the old man's eyes. "Curiosity is the child's plaything, Thomas. Becoming a man one must leave childish things behind. Is it not you now who are seeking beyond what is present, or real? It takes great effort to understand what we already know, what we already have."

"I don't understand that. Why shouldn't I know who is here with us?"

Duban patted the back of the soldier's hand. "And why should you? You know so very little of this world, our world. You are here, hopefully for your own sake, not much longer. You know nothing of our allies, who are nearer than you think and frequently attend here. Even less of the insurgents and enemies who may not be much further away."

"Perhaps when I manage to remember everything. I must know something about such things. I was – am – a soldier."

"Very true. Perhaps you will know more than we do. I imagine your gradual recovery keeps you safe from the information. I cannot explain to you everything about the lives of my niece and I. Furthermore I am not persuaded that it would benefit you, or us, in any way. We wish to see you healed, and returned to your own life. We will do everything in our power to help you, believe me my friend." He took his hand away. "The radio. Have you done more work on it?"

Haldane knew there was no point in pressing the matter further. "Whatever my duties were on that helicopter working the radio, or doing anything with the electrics, weren't part of them. Either that or my memory's even worse than I thought. But I did notice there is what I think must be a battery, inside the thing. If we could find a replacement, or a way of charging it, then that would be a step forward."

"Let me think about that. We should be getting a visit from our friends outside soon, I would have thought. Give me the old battery if you can, and we shall see what we can do. Now, Captain – eat and rest!"

Haldane did eat but decided not to rest. He was curious about the woman he saw. He would scout the gardens and the paths back to the house. Whoever she was she must come home eventually, and her quarters could only be in some part of the buildings. There was nowhere else inside the barbed high walls for her to rest and shelter.

Twice now he had tried to open the heavy doors at the old main entrance. They were not simply locked but looked out of use for many years, barred and bolted, boarded up. So far he had only seen two other ways of entering and leaving the house – through the French windows of the great chamber or the little doorway he had just discovered at Ma'ahaba's herb garden. Perhaps the mysterious woman used that route. But now, exploring the porch between the pillars he noticed that, next to the ancient doors was a smaller side door. He had seen that before, but on closer inspection there was a door within a door. Not deliberately concealed – there was a substantial enough handle on it – but just not obvious to the stranger. He pushed on the handle and thought at first that it was locked too. Applying more force didn't budge it, but tinkering with the angle of what must be a loose latch, eventually the handle turned and the door opened.

Haldane stepped inside. Although, he calculated, he couldn't be as much as a hundred yards from the part of the house he already knew – a wall or two separating them – he felt as if he was in a completely different dwelling. There were settles and ottomans, what looked like a church pew, at the foot of a grand staircase. The steps were not in the middle but curled up the left hand side of the hall. To the right of them the hall itself extended into the gloom, but he could see a couple of doors. One, he gauged, must lead, somehow, through to the newer part of the building with the great room, the library, dining room and up to his own quarters. The other, presumably, towards where he had seen Ma'ahaba reading and out onto the herb garden.

He decided to climb the stairs, but not without some hesitation. The place did not alarm him, despite its austerity and dusty silence. But because, again, he felt he was sticking his nose where it did not belong. Perhaps Duban was right. Why try and uncover information that was of no direct use to him? Duban and his niece were looking after him to the best of their ability, keeping him safe from murderous rebels, and helping him escape. If indeed there were mysteries in their home, and an inmate was being kept from him, then they would have their reasons. Yet something else clicked into place in his head. Something, he thought, that may have to do with his military training. A need to understand the lie of the land, calculate possibilities and threats. So he mounted the stairs slowly.

There were more portraits on the wall, ascending the stairs. All men, some in army uniforms not unlike his own, some in ceremonial robes, a few with hats similar to that which Duban wore but more decorative. They shared a clear family resemblance. Handsome faces, or at least once handsome – they all seemed to have been painted in the later stages of life, once they had earned respect and fame. High forehead, brown hair, deep-set eyes. They had all been painted by the same hand, though that was not possible – judging by their clothes, and by the age of the canvases and frames, these men were spread across centuries. Each of them had been told to look directly at the artist, and they were all deadly serious. This perpetual painter was not, to Haldane's mind, particularly gifted. He hadn't managed to catch the individuality or life in any of his subjects. Their eyes seemed as dead as the alabaster sockets in the statues outside. A series of portrayals of a single self-important, mirthless bully.

As he made his way up he thought he heard a sound similar to that he'd been hearing at night – a rhythmic whisper. But he couldn't trust his own ears. The sound was so quiet and seemed too distant even for a house this size. He stopped just before he reached the upper landing. Like the hall below there were pieces of furniture, more family portraits, unlit candles and lamps. The whispering, if he'd heard it at all, seemed even further off now. Perhaps it was simply a draft somewhere below. Feeling ever more ashamed for his invasion into a private family space he stepped up onto the landing and made his way towards the first door, to his left.

If he opened it, what would he find? An empty room which wasn't his to be in. Or, conceivably, the mystery woman who clearly did not want him there.

He felt he had done enough for the moment. He had found the other – and greater – part of the house, and the probable location of the woman. No need to rush things. He made his way downstairs as quickly and as lightly as he could. Just as he was stepping out into the heat of the late afternoon, he thought he heard someone speak. Gently, and at some distance. It occurred to him that if you could hear a smile that would be its sound. He realised he had been tense, exploring the secret house, but that sound put him at his ease again.

Back in his room, after opening the radio up and managing to remove the dud battery, he lay on his bed, the open window offering no cooling breeze. Closing his eyes he saw the face of his father.

"He who is lost to shame, is lost."

Whether it was a memory of his father actually saying these words or he was half-dreaming them, Haldane couldn't say. In his mind's eye he was standing in front of his father's desk, with its piles of books and papers, his collection of sermons in their red ring binder, and Haldane remembered now what the argument was about. It was the day he had told his father that he had decided to join the army. A decision that he had known full well would astound and distress the older man. But whatever words passed between them were drowned now by the sound of a helicopter plunging, engine grinding, and men crying.

When he woke, dusk thickening, he found that the bandage on his leg had been changed.

The Maid's Tale

Haldane sat in the clearing where he had first seen Ma'ahaba sunning her thighs and shoulders. There was a little stone bench there, beside a softly flowing channel of the irrigation system, warmed already by the morning sun. He closed his eyes and heard her voice for the first time.

"You will go away."

At first he thought he was dreaming again. The voice was so delicate and the words faint and feathery that perhaps Duban was right, he was hearing the air speak. He turned around, without knowing in which direction to look, for the words seemed to have come out of nowhere. He stood up and held his hand over his eyes, the sun blinding him.

There was no one there. No movement, other than the usual swaying of branches and flitting of birds. He moved towards where he had thought the words came from. A group of high bushes or rushes. Though perhaps they hadn't come from there, but from the more formal line of fruit trees. It made no difference. Everywhere he looked there was nothing to suggest that anyone had been there. The words, it seemed, had come out of nowhere.

That night he was invited into the dining room again to eat with Duban and Ma'ahaba. Haldane decided not to speak of what he had heard, or believed he had heard. Not because he might anger Duban and Ma'ahaba, though that concerned him too, or that they might question his sanity, but because the voice now seemed like his secret as well as theirs. Or a different secret altogether.

"You changed my bandage, Duban. While I slept. Thank you."

"Not last night, Thomas. The bandage was changed a day or so ago. You must only have noticed it today."

"Strange. It worries me that I have no memory of it whatsoever. Doesn't bode well for my convalescence."

"Or perhaps it is simply a tribute to my ministry," Duban said, glowing.

"You seemed to be at least half awake, Captain," Ma'ahaba said as, this time, Duban served her.

"You were there too?"

"Merely to assist the physician. Duban tended to you, I held the water and the ointment." She held up her palms in innocence. "I promise I did not touch you."

"Well, thank you both. I apologise for being in such a dwam all the time."

"You've been busy too, Thomas! You retrieved the battery from the radio and you've managed to make a few other little repairs on the apparatus. I had a look while we bandaged you. We spoke about it, but you were, it is true, a little dazed."

"I got the impression," Ma'ahaba said softly, "that your home situation is not unlike my own."

"Ma'ab. No need to pester our guest with that."

"I'm sorry. How do you mean?"

"You live, or at least did until I'd say relatively recently, with an older man, who was holy and wise and whom you respected but did not always agree with. Out in the country, no? With few like-minded people within easy reach. Probably, though, our lives are in stark contrast. The moment you could, you got out. To find adventure in the big world. Whereas I sang and danced in the world but returned."

"And perhaps Thomas will do the same."

"Hopefully," Haldane spoke to Ma'ahaba, "the war will end, and you can resume your life."

"I said nothing, Captain, of my life being halted."

Duban spoke before he could answer. "When you speak of your early life, Thomas, you never mention your mother. Only your father."

"Now that you mention it. I can see him clearly. But not her. That's surprising, isn't it?"

Ma'ahaba laughed. "Perhaps you're a man's man. You became a soldier after all."

The next morning Haldane returned to the little stone bench in the clearing and positioned himself exactly as he had done the day before. Time passed but no voice came out of the trees or the air. Thinking back he worried. He had heard nothing. Or, worse, he had misheard – she, whoever she was, had said "Go away" and not "You will go away." The phantom voice was unhappy with him, troubled by his presence. He was not welcome here.

And then he wondered if the voice, just possibly, now that it was so faint in his memory, could have been Ma'ahaba's? That possibility hadn't occurred to him at the time. It sounded nothing like her and anyway why would she hide herself from him. If it was indeed Ma'ahaba, then that at least solved the mystery. But the idea saddened him. Because it meant there was no mystery: the world was just the way it seemed and there was nothing more to discover. And because he had grown to like Ma'ahaba very much.

His neck began to ache. He closed his eyes, and slumbered. A dreamless sleep, not even darkness. Not even nothing; no awareness of nothingness.

He woke with a jump, and wondered how long he had been out for. He had been fast asleep, that was sure, because he found it difficult to wake himself properly. His sight was blurrier than ever, his limbs heavy and bloodless. When he managed to look up the sun seemed to be in precisely the same position it had been before he had dropped off. But he felt he had slept for some hours. Was it possible an entire day had passed? His memory was shot. If he couldn't remember Duban and Ma'ahaba dressing his wounds then it was also possible he had lived out the entire previous day but couldn't now bring it to mind.

His energy returning, he shook his head and scolded himself. Obviously he had simply dozed for a few minutes. But as he walked out from the clearing in the copse he heard the voice again.

"Soon."

And this time he was sterner with himself. Such a short word, it could indeed be the rustling of leaves, or the water playing over stones in the stream. Yet he felt he had heard it so clearly. Soon.

He returned to where he had been and scanned the area, turning a full 360 degrees, alert to every movement, every bird on every branch. The sun was still strong. Blinking and narrowing his eyes, looking over to his left he found her.

She was standing a few yards deeper into the garden, beside a tree, its branches and yellow fruits fanning and half-concealing her. She was, as he'd glimpsed her before, mistaking her for Ma'ahaba, dressed all in white, a cowl over her hair and her neck and lips veiled. He had no idea what he should say to her, nor whether he should approach or remain seated. After a moment, the woman spoke again.

"My name is Aliyyah."

"Captain Haldane, at your service."

Aliyyah laughed, just as he had heard her do in the house: the sound of a smile, of mildness. She stepped out from behind the boughs of the tree. "I have been watching you."

"And I have been trying to find you."

"I know." And this time when she laughed he heard the family resemblance – although the laugh of a young woman it reminded him of old Duban's merry giggle.

"Will you get into trouble?" he asked.

"Are you worried that I might? Or that you might, Captain Haldane."

"You're right. Both, I suppose. Your... family, have been very kind to me. I don't wish to upset them."

"But not enough to refrain from prowling and prying?"

"I'm sorry," he said though he had detected no hint of criticism in her tone.

Now that she had taken another step or two towards him, Haldane stood and got the measure of her a little more. She was young, yes, but not a girl. Perhaps only a couple of years younger than himself. The wisps he could see of her hair were chestnut brown, and her eyes the most striking green. The green of a forest in late summer. Her brows arched, inquisitive. And though she kept the mantle on below her eyes it was diaphanous enough for him to see that her expression was calm.

She dropped her head for a moment, then turned to go.

"Aliyyah? Am I to say that I have met you?"

She considered this briefly, her brows furrowing. "I see no point in lying."

"And will I see you again?"

"That would be pleasant, Captain."

When she had gone he was left only with the echo of her voice, like water, he thought, running over smooth stones.

"Aliyyah introduced herself to me today." Haldane was working on the radio, but absent-mindedly, not really attempting to fix it, when Duban had knocked and entered his room.

"So she said," Duban replied and Haldane could not detect whether the old man disapproved or not. But it was unusual for Duban to come to his quarters or to seek him out.

"Why was she such a big secret?"

"No secret, my friend. Just the way we live here. If

Aliyyah decided that the two of you should meet, then that is a matter for herself."

With that the old man turned and left the room. Some minutes later Haldane followed him down and found him in his library, searching the lower shelves, until he found the book he was looking for. At the back of the room there was a tiny window, round like a porthole. Ma'ahaba was standing there, looking out into the falling night.

"So we may speak, Aliyyah and I, without either of us getting into trouble?"

Ma'ahaba laughed. "You sound like a child," she said without turning round. There was, Haldane knew, displeasure in the way she stood, one arm around her own waist, the other smoothing her hair.

"You are free to come and go in our house, Thomas." Duban's expression relaxed a little, "I imagine you will not have much time to spend together."

Whether he meant the soldier's departure was imminent or that Aliyyah would not make, or be given, time for him, Haldane chose not to ask.

"Nor do I think," Ma'ahaba opened the door to the gardens, "that the two of you will be good for each other." And she stepped out.

The following morning Haldane was on his way back again to the clearing, but he saw that Ma'ahaba had beaten him to the spot. Like the first time he had seen her, she seemed dead to the world, her head resting on a tree behind her, eyes closed, thighs and shoulders exposed to the sun, breathing deeply. And again, as he turned away, he thought he caught her smiling, perhaps smirking, aware of his presence and his eyes.

Striking what he thought might be eastwards into the orchard along a path he could not remember walking before, he arrived at an old fountain. There he sat and he waited, and before long he heard Aliyyah in the trees behind him. She was singing quietly, to herself, and in a tongue Haldane did not recognise. Soft vowels over sharp consonants. Then, at the end of her song, as she neared, he understood a few words… "The captain whose soldiers are blossoms."

She was dressed just as she had been the day before, and this time she stepped closer to him.

"Will you sit, Aliyyah?"

"Yes," she replied but did not move.

The scarf round her neck – made of silk or chiffon, Haldane didn't know – was so fine that though it covered her lips he could see her expression and at the moment she had, he thought, the faintest of smiles.

"I feel I ought to make conversation," Haldane said, "but knowing so little about you, or even if I should talk to you at all, makes it difficult."

"Isn't there something civilised about pauses in conversation? It means we are thinking."

Haldane laughed. "In order to pause don't you need to begin?"

Aliyyah turned away and walked towards the trees she had appeared from. But she stopped and turned her head and he understood it to mean that he was to follow. Walking a few paces in front of him, Aliyyah asked: "Where do you come from, Captain?"

"You are like Ma'ahaba. Insisting on titles."

Without turning she repeated, "Where do you come from, Thomas?"

"Tom. My friends call me Tom." He smiled, "but I'm not sure I ever liked it."

"Then I shall call you Tom! What is Tom's land?"

"I was raised in a place called Shaws."

"I had heard your memory was bad."

"Only for some things. Especially what brought me here."

"The only journey is the one within," Aliyyah said and laughed happily, as if remembering something.

"You sound like your uncle."

At last Aliyyah stopped. Beside a little fountain, still in working order, the clear water splashing gently into a basin surrounded by miniature stone lions holding up a stone shelf that served as a seat. She sat at one end, leaving space for Haldane.

"And you, Aliyyah. Were you raised here, in this house?"

"I have been to the town," and she nodded past his shoulder, northwards. "But not much further. The war began when I was little."

"There is a town?" Haldane surprised himself with the question, and looked behind him. It felt rude, when he should have sympathised with her being a victim of the war.

"A day's walk away. Although I remember my father driving there when I was very little and it seemed to take only minutes."

"You've been cooped up here all your life?"

"Cooped up?"

He had become so used to Duban's and Ma'ahaba's excellent English that it hadn't occurred to him there would be gaps in their, or Aliyyah's, knowledge of the language. "Closed in. Confined."

"I do not feel confined."

"A young woman like you?"

"The war will end. I have my uncle. And Ma'ahaba. I have many things."

"Ma'ahaba. She is your mother?"

Aliyyah laughed cheerfully. "I hope you have not asked her that! She is much younger than her sister who was my mother. We feel, Ma'ahaba and I, that we are the sisters now."

"Then where is your mother?"

She fixed him with her green eyes. "No one knows. We must assume she is dead now. But perhaps when the war is over... She disappeared one day, when I was very little. In the early years of the fighting. There was a skirmish here. Perhaps she was taken, by one side or

"…a little fountain, the clear water splashing gently into a basin
surrounded by miniature stone lions"

the other. Or perhaps she was killed that day and her remains spirited away."

"I'm sorry."

"I am too. But nothing ever goes away completely. No one vanishes into thin air. It's true, isn't it, that matter never goes away, it changes, but doesn't… unmaterialise. Everything there is, all that we see around us, is only there because of what went before. What it grew out of."

"I suppose. But losing you mother is still hard."

"I don't just mean atoms and particles. Where do words go once they are spoken? They vibrate in the air, do they not? And thin out, disperse. All the words ever spoken are all around us now, like the birdsong we're hearing. Including my mother's words. The words she spoke to me, though I cannot remember them."

"It's a beautiful idea."

"And perhaps, though we do not know the science of it yet, the same is true of every caress, and every thought." Aliyyah smiled. "I know what you are thinking, soldier man. Then the same must be true of every insult and blow and hateful thought. Well perhaps that is the arrangement. The covenant."

"Perhaps it is. I'm not sure what I make of that. But you still have your father? General Deimos? What happened after his wife disappeared?"

"He asked his sister-in-law to return from her studies to help with me. Some years later they married. And very soon after he was called to the capital and has been unable to return much since."

"It's a terrible situation."

"Ma'ahaba has adapted I think. And this is all I know. Or, for the moment at least, want."

"But you must dream of leaving? Seeing the world, finding friends…"

"Friends and the world lie beyond a curtain of bullets and bombs and hatred. I fear that more than I need them." She paused. "No, not fear. Or not mostly fear. Life is short. I would rather remain here in peace. I have much to do here."

"Like what?"

"I have my lessons to complete with Duban. I have songs still to learn, and those I already know to perfect. I understand so little."

"What does Duban instruct you in?"

"Everything."

"English? He's done a good job."

"We speak, all three of us, some days only in your language, some days in others. Days can go by without uttering a word in my own tongue."

"What else does Duban teach you?"

"Knowledge, of all kinds. Although I believe that knowledge lies in the soul, like a seed in the soil. A teacher brings light, learning is the flower. But this is boring, Tom."

"Not at all. I'm fascinated."

"I'm not," and he saw under the silk her teasing smile.

"Just as I cannot claim to be a physician nor would I profess to be a teacher." Duban and Haldane were sitting outside the great chamber, a plate of supper in their hands. "In her words, Aliyyah and I learn about many things together. Knowing one's own ignorance is the best part of knowledge, Thomas, don't you agree? Only a fool has found wisdom, the wise seek it."

The time between being with Aliyyah and being with Duban had somehow evaporated. How she had left him, and how the old man had found him was unclear. The dull ache had returned and the soldier felt tired. All he could remember of the walk back to the house was his blurry vision giving a creamy, faded aspect to the trees and fruits and the ground beneath his feet.

"You say you are a priest, Duban."

"It is the title you used, I believe. And it seems to…

impede you in some way. You know that it derives from an ancient word meaning old man," Duban threw up his arms and cackled. "In which case I am most certainly a priest!"

"Of what creed?"

"Of the creed of this land, of my people. But in the end all creeds are the same. All those that ponder the Divine and wish to know it."

"So you and Ma'ahaba and Aliyyah are all religious?"

"The manner in which you say it, Thomas… I detect a displeasure?"

"You shouldn't. Though I have no religion myself."

"Of course you do my friend. We all do. No one can wake and negotiate the day without a degree of faith. If only that death will not happen today. The most rational of us ignores on a daily basis the one fact – a fact!" Duban clapped his hands gleefully, "That we know to be immutably true. We will die. This moment or the next."

"I don't see how that is religion."

"It is a problematic word. Let's talk instead of a set of decisions, of observances, that help guide our steps, and how we read the world around us. Are you, for instance, like Plato believing that the almond tree there is not the real almond tree but its shadow? Or that it vanishes the moment you turn your gaze? Even without knowing it you have taken decisions on the nature of things in order to live."

"But a priest judges the world according to some higher power."

"And you do not? Even in the unlikely event that mankind, as a whole, reaches complete understanding of the cosmos, no one man can possess and compute all the necessary information. Therefore you have faith in the teachings of others – those who decipher signs and language and systems beyond your ken – most of them dead now, and mix them with your own experience of the world."

"They are not the same thing."

"Are they not?" Duban looked genuinely concerned. "We like to think that we humans are struggling to reach our true destiny. Peace and understanding. Progress. It is a form of redemption, don't you think, Thomas? An idea that is dear to people like me – and which you have borrowed from people like me."

"I'm not looking for any redemption, Duban."

The older man stopped smiling, put his palms together and waited for Haldane to explain, his old eyes shining like a child's. "But you think, I am sure, that humans are the highest of animals. Take away the divine, and humanity itself departs. All you have done is replace the Mystery with a flattering image of us."

"By that reckoning, Duban, anyone could defend any madness."

Duban looked crestfallen. "And you, I ask again, do not? Defend your madness. It is you, Captain, who are fighting this war, not I. Beyond these gates, Madness reigns."

"Half the reason – no, more than half – for this damn war is people believing crazy things."

"Ah but which ones are crazy? I grant you, terrible things have been done in the name of piety. On the other hand I do not contend that the gun is the fault of science."

They spoke for a while more, Haldane, as in the memories of the argument with his father, hearing the sounds both men were making but not the words. His own voice sounded confident and calm, as did Duban's, but where their conversation led them he couldn't tell.

Recon. The word came back to him as he lay in his bed, the room infused with ambergris or some aroma that reminded him of incense in chapels. His job – in the army not the air force – was recon. Reconnaissance. He knew – though he couldn't recall any of it now – a lot about weather and terrain. And about equipment, though apparently not radios.

Most of his time in the base camp, he was sure, was spent writing reports, communiqués, calculations.

He hadn't thought they were overly deep into enemy territory the day Michael and… Simon! That was it. The door gunner. Simon, and Mick the pilot. They were laughing about something. It couldn't be they had flown over this actual house? He had an image in his head of seeing a woman lying in a clearing, sunning herself. Was that what had cheered them up and had them joking and laughing? He was getting things mixed up, surely.

And then there was a noise, not an explosion. More like when a car prangs. Nothing too alarming. Had something gone wrong with the engine? There was no one below that he could remember who could have hit them with bullets or shells. But the engine noise kept changing and their laughter turned to looks of concern, Michael anxiously pushing buttons and pulling levers. At first the 'copter seemed to float upwards. Then it swooped, swirling them about inside, throwing them around in their seats. Haldane thought maybe his safety belt had come undone. There was shouting, a rush of wind as a door opened somewhere. Did Simon jump out? Was he shouting at them to do the same?

And then the plunging. Not just falling but being sucked down. And into darkness, though it must still have been daytime. Not dropping but being pulled, as if some force below, some beast, below even the ground itself, was reaching up and grabbing them, tearing them from the sky.

Haldane's skin froze as he remembered. And the ache in his neck, from his head being forced back into his seat, returned with a vengeance. He tried to summon up the image he had dreamed of Ma'ahaba taking the reigns and driving them out of their fall and back up into the air, but she would not come. He tried imagining Aliyyah there instead, but the terror of the lurching, the headlong dive, the suction from under the earth, obliterated everything else in his mind. He was shivering on his bed, violently, like a fit, and he thought that, if he should have died then, he was going to now instead. Then there was darkness. Like oil, crude and stinking, devouring, decomposing him, until he was no longer there. Not in his bed, or in the infinite blackness. Just a knowledge that in that nothingness there was the idea of him, somewhere in the wide darkness.

Just before he woke, or as he was waking, the darkness seemed to change. Soft, velvety. Then the smell of pear, pomegranate, and he opened his eyes to his white walls and the window with the single green tree and its crimson blooms.

Aliyyah and Haldane walked the path that led back from the old entrance to the main gate. He saw now that no path had ever been laid in brick or tarmac but simply a dust track that had been stamped and hardened by the traverse of boots and shoes over many many years.

"I heard you singing."

"Oh, I try and practice far enough away for no one to hear. I am not very good."

"I'm sure you are. But, yes, it was in the distance so I couldn't hear well. It sounded charming. What do you sing?"

"Old songs and new songs. Mainly old songs. Since we lost power here I cannot listen to new songs. There is an old gramophone so now I have to learn my songs from there."

"Songs in your own language? Or would I know any of them?"

Aliyyah stopped for a moment and thought.

"Be happy, relax. Cares eat away at the heart. Abandon this and live in happiness."

This time she dared to sing a little louder, an energy and decisiveness in her voice. Only a line or two but as she sang her mantilla fell from her mouth and he watched entranced as her lips moved, but only just, her eyes peering into the trees, glistening.

"The sun has gazed upon me. Now dawn has appeared."

Where before the soldier had thought the young woman bonny he now felt her beauty; it tightened his chest and seemed, suddenly, like a barrier between them. Her voice dropped off and she looked at him and gave him a broad, happy smile, before casually replacing her shawl and walking on.

The path was longer than he remembered and they strolled on far beyond the point he had expected to arrive at the gate. She recited scraps of poems, mostly in her own tongue, and then she insisted that he too must know some songs or rhymes.

"I don't think it's my memory," he laughed, "I'm fairly certain I'm a terrible singer. Poems...?" One came to mind though he didn't know where he had learned it. "I see her in the dewy flowers, I see her sweet and fair: I hear her in the tuneful birds, I hear her charm the air."

Aliyyah was delighted. "Did you make that up for me?"

"God, no. I wish. I imagine I'm a worse poet than a singer. It's an old song, I think, though I can't remember the tune."

At points the track became rough and stony and once Aliyyah, wearing only brightly beaded slippers, stumbled and allowed Haldane to steady her, their hands clasping for a moment.

"Why are we walking here?" she asked. "It is the least pretty part of the grounds. Beauty is like goodness, don't you think, Tom? The nearer we get to the gates the more ugly everything becomes."

Turning the next bend they arrived at last at the gate itself. "But it's also beautiful – out there. Those mountains. The... bigness, the openness of it all."

Aliyyah stared out at the vast landscape beyond the bars of the gate, stopping and standing still.

"Do you think they know they are there?"

"What? The mountains?" Haldane burst out laughing. "I have never heard anyone talk the way you do, Aliyyah. Not even your uncle."

At the mention of Duban, Aliyyah furrowed her brow. "I should go back. I hate to keep him waiting." She turned and quickened her step down the narrow lane, Haldane following on.

"What is your lesson this afternoon?"

She did not turn but spoke with her back to him. "A book, I think, he wants to show me. One I've never seen before."

"What kind of a book? Is he training you for something?"

At that she glanced round. "What could he possibly be training me for?"

"I don't know. But he is instructing you in his beliefs."

"We talk. We consider. And we read. Yes, I learn from him. And, yes, Duban has a particular wisdom, that stretches back to ancient times, if that is what you mean?"

Arriving at the old porch, which came upon them much sooner than he'd expected, Aliyyah turned to the soldier. He thought she might take a step towards him but she remained still. Instead he advanced and bent his head towards her, the fabric of her veil soft on his skin like a whisper.

That evening, at table, Ma'ahaba sat and let Haldane serve her from a ready-prepared salver of leaves and nuts and spices.

"It seems that Duban has been waylaid this evening, Captain," and she smiled, "you have been left alone with me." It registered with him that this was most definitely a family. They shared certain expressions and gestures, and of course their accents were similar, though fainter in Ma'ahaba's case. "Does that discomfort you?"

"Not at all. Why should it?"

54

"A fighting man like you, unused to female company other than canteen ladies, I imagine."

"Women are soldiers now too."

"So I've heard. A great woman once said, 'Give a girl the right shoes and she'll conquer the world. So now it's combat boots.'"

"You disapprove, Ma'ahaba?"

"Wasn't there a woman warrior from your land? One who mustered men for battle? Only everyone then said she was merely the consort of the king, a foolish woman in love."

"I don't know the story."

They ate for a moment in silence. "So how do you find my stepdaughter, Captain?"

"She's very lovely. But I can't pretend to understand her."

"Oh, I wouldn't try to do that. With anyone."

"Why doesn't she dine with us? Is it because I am here? She would normally?"

"No doubt your presence will have a certain influence. Though whether it's you yourself or just the appearance of someone unexpected is debatable."

Ma'ahaba leaned forward and smiled. "May I change the subject for a moment? For my own part I'm delighted to have someone new here for a while. But I should point out something a little delicate to you…" She put her hand to her mouth, girlishly. "While you were comatose, Duban nursed you and washed you. The night we changed your bandages we refreshed you again. But that's a day or two ago now. Forgive me for pointing out… there is by the east side of the house a fountain that serves as a shower. There are several but that is the nearest to your room." Ma'ahaba laughed. "It is not entirely dislikable, Captain, but even soldierly muskiness should be regulated."

Embarrassed, Haldane sought out that night the fountain

she referred to. Exiting by the door of the great chamber and turning immediately right then right again and behind an old wall he'd thought was the remainder of some old outhouse, there was indeed a taller font than any he had seen before. A basic, rough stone, unadorned like the other springs and bowls and decorations around the gardens. Being dark and concealed behind the old wall he thought it safe to strip and wash thoroughly. The jets of water, however, were clearly designed for display and not for bathing. Most of the water splashed wide of him and only a sharp single stream fell directly on his head. He had no soap and he realised that not only was his hair longer now than army regulation but that his beard had grown. What a disagreeable presence he must be! And though still wincing at Ma'ahaba pointing out his deterioration he found himself laughing at her mocking and teasing remarks, saying she was worried they were running out of sweet-smelling oils for his room.

It was the first time he'd laughed out loud since the accident, and he felt both guilt and release. The cold water was invigorating on his skin and he felt a freedom in his nakedness and solitude. The stars above mingled with the shards and droplets of water so that it seemed he was bathing in the Milky Way itself, shimmering in glittering light.

He spoke to Duban the following day of the sensation. "Do you know the story," the old man asked, "of Juno? There are many different versions, but here is one. Juno was the mother of Mars and Vulcan. But she was also the saviour of Heracles. After completing his trials the warrior, exhausted, lay dying. But Juno came down from the heavens to suckle him at her breast, thus turning him from weak mortal into eternal deity. Some drops of milk spilled whilst she was nursing him. And those are the stars we see now. Truly the Milky Way!"

"You know a lot of odd things, Duban!"

They were sitting inside the chamber looking out on a dusty day. Since early morning the day had seemed cloudy – still dry and hot, but as if a fog had gathered. The dregs of a sandstorm, the reconnaissance officer had worked out, probably blowing high up among the mountains somewhere.

"Knowledge is a useful vessel, my son, but it needs a skillful driver, else it might take you nowhere in particular." Duban was standing looking out on the brownish, hazy orchard. But now he came and sat close by Haldane's side. "We must speak about Aliyyah, Thomas."

"Ah."

"I have still known you longer as a sleeping man than a wakened one, but I think I can make a judgement. You are honourable, that is certain. But also I think perhaps tenacious? Would that be the right word?"

"I'm not sure. I seem to be making a slow recovery. And I admit to having felt a lack of resolve. But I think that is changing now."

"I am glad to hear it. It is possible that tonight we will be visited by our friends on the outside."

"How can you know that?"

"I do not know, Thomas. But dull, sooty days like this are not, I have gathered, ideal for fighting. Restricted visibility et cetera et cetera et cetera? I have noticed a certain pattern and while the dust is settling our companions often arrive. But I may be wrong."

"You were talking about Aliyyah."

"And I will come straight to the point. Your comportment with her I know will be exemplary... as far as you can be aware. But you must know that your presence here is a major event in her young life."

"Young. How old is she, Duban? She's not a girl."

"She is, she can only be, given her cloistered life here, younger than her years. Cloistered, I should say, by events, not by any person's will –"

"I reckon she must be… twenty? And are you sure that she is not being kept here by the will of others? Instead of posting you and Ma'ahaba to look after her here her father could have brought her to the city. Or sent her somewhere safe."

"This is the safest place the General knows, Thomas."

"My memory of the details of the war are vague, but I think it's likely to be a long one. So many years confined to a single house? However pretty its gardens are."

"This is what I feared." Duban looked directly at him and his eyes clouded over. "You want to make changes, revisions in the lives of others, without knowing much about them."

"I'm suggesting no such thing, Duban. We are just talking, and I'm telling you truthfully what I think."

"I thank you for your forthrightness. Naturally there is no restriction on thinking."

"Isn't there? Are there restrictions on Aliyyah's thinking?"

"Even if one were to wish it, we cannot control what goes on inside people's heads."

"And do you wish it?"

"You mean as her counsellor? I think we all wish the best for those whom we love and if we could prevent damaging actions and thoughts we would. But we could talk for many days about such matters and, much as I enjoy our conversations, time is running out."

The old man got up from his seat with, Haldane noted, admirable ease. He moved, it occurred to him now, with the fluidity of a much younger man.

"And that is why it is so important that you do not unsettle Aliyyah too much. You will be gone presently. Back to your life. A world fundamentally different from hers. We all fervently hope that this war will end sooner rather than later so that we can continue with our lives in peace. But that is not going to happen soon. The danger for you here is as great as the danger for her out there. By all means delight in your time together, but do not imperil one another."

Haldane got up. "You're warning me off?"

"That," Duban said sadly, "is a churlish interpretation of what I have just said, and not worthy of you, Captain."

The soldier and the girl found new regions of the gardens to explore, places where the walls and barbed wire could not be seen, or even brought to mind. The air was still grainy but the heat, as evening approached, abated. The whole orchard was a study in gentle browns and yellows; the fruits, yesterday so red and gaudy, were today rose-hued and the trees and boughs delicate filigree. Aliyyah's eyes, normally deep burning green, reminded him now of the briars and mosses of his native land.

"So you believe in nothing?" she looked at him, fascinated, after he told her that he had given up on his father's faith. "Strange."

"Why?"

"It sounds... magical. This nothingness of yours. I can hardly even imagine it. Look – everything's here. There are bits of nothing, I suppose, in the spaces there, between that tree and that one. But I know that it isn't really nothing. There's nitrogen and oxygen and carbon dioxide in there. Where is your nothing?"

"I think what Duban has taught you best is riddles, Aliyyah! Like him you have a way of turning things on their head."

"I think he is right. That you, and those of like mind, are the most mystical of all. The holy books say beautiful things like, 'In the beginning was the Word and the Word was made flesh,' and 'The heavens and earth once were one until torn asunder.' Oh and I like 'Nor aught nor naught existed; no confine twixt day and night.' Strange words, I agree. But yours – 'In the beginning there was nothing, and everything was born of nothing.' That one I find hardest to understand."

"Only because Duban decides what you should read and how you should think."

She looked at him with mock anger: "Do you really think me such a foolish girl, Tom?"

"Not at all," he laughed. "You're cleverer than me and have had more time to think. But we're all limited by what we've learned and who does the teaching."

"All of us? You too?"

"I suppose."

"The critic always looks for faults," she laughed.

"And the faithful for excuses."

She skipped ahead of him. "Enough. Tell me about the places you've been. Cities! Have you been to many cities?"

"Yes. Though like everything else they're a bit fuzzy in my head." They sat down together on the ground under a willow tree. "The city nearest to me when I was growing up. Quite a small city really. I think you would like it there, Aliyyah. The stone is sometimes milky, when it's sunny, sometimes silvery, in the smir."

"Smir?"

"When it rains very softly. There are old streets, like in stories, winding and turning. And new gleaming ones with shops and restaurants and life and noise. You would definitely like it."

"I would. And books? There will be so many books."

"Just about everything that's ever been written, I guess. Libraries and bookshops. And dress shops with every kind of fashion you can imagine. And gardens, with plants from all over the world."

"Then why did you leave?"

"To see what other places are like?"

"And you found a broken old house in the middle of a messy old garden," she laughed.

"Going out into the world you learn."

"Or do you just carry what you already know with you everywhere?"

"You would learn all kinds of things in my country."

"There are so many things I do not know even here, in front of my eyes. What is that little flower there? I've seen it so many times, yet it has no name for me. I read of a man once, who saw a flower. Perhaps one just like that. He sat down to study it, and became entranced. When finally the spell was broken he found a hundred years had passed." She smiled directly at Haldane. "Or perhaps it was ten. I don't remember. Or perhaps I dreamed the whole story up."

They wandered through the wood for some time more, looking for trees and grasses and fruits, exchanging their names for them. Tulip, fig, rose and quince. Her words for the same things sounded spacious, rippling – more like, Haldane thought, the things themselves. When neither of them knew the name in either language they invented one between them, hybrid words. "Shanitha!" "Flomerah." "Distãn!"

That evening, having walked Aliyyah to the old main door, Haldane strolled a little longer by himself through the dusk. He heard voices that at first he assumed came from the great chamber. But passing it, a few lamps and tapers still flickering, he saw there was no one there. The voices were somewhere outside, beyond the old wall that concealed the shower fountain. He ventured further in that direction, quickly picking up a path that he calcu-lated must branch off from the dust road that led back to the porch and main door. The voices were further from the house, however, and Haldane followed the sound. He assumed he was hearing Duban and Ma'ahaba, discussing something happily.

Night falling fast now, he tripped once or twice on roots and stones and scratched his finger on a thorn. To one side the wall loomed darkly behind bushes and trees and this new path followed its contour. Turning a gradual bend he saw a light emerging from an opening in the centre of a copse of trees. At first he thought it must be a camp-fire. Closer still he could make out the silhouette of a man, lit but not by flames. The light didn't flicker but still came from the ground around the man's feet. Little glowing oblong pools, like fairy lights. The man was sitting, but even so Haldane could see he was much bulkier than Duban. The soldier's protective instincts kicked in and he crouched low, studying the terrain in front of him, picking a line of least resistance to get nearer without being seen or heard.

The stranger was dressed in the outfit that many of the subjects of the portraits wore: a round cap, khaki shirt with gun belt and some kind of tabard over his shoulders. Next to him, at the edge of the faint but steady light given out by those strange little rectangles, Haldane thought he could make out a rifle, lying against the bench or rock the man was sitting on.

He was talking calmly, telling a story, but to whom, Haldane couldn't see. The story didn't seem particularly important or serious, the man at ease and comfortable in his surroundings. Haldane decided not to risk getting any closer – whether there was any danger or not he couldn't be certain – but moved to one side trying to see who the stranger was talking to. And just as he saw her, as she leaned into the mysterious gloaming and he glimpsed her covered face, thinking at once she was Aliyyah, the woman and the soldier burst into loud laughter. Ma'ahaba – for it was she – immediately put her finger to her face to subdue the man's guffaws, but still chuckling herself.

There was an easy familiarity about them. As if all she wanted was not to disturb anyone trying to sleep rather than keeping their meeting clandestine. When their laughter subsided Ma'ahaba spoke in her language to the

"The light didn't flicker but still came from the ground around the man's feet. Little glowing oblong pools, like fairy lights."

visitor and she made no attempt to keep her voice low. The man leaned in closer to her, listening, and once, perhaps to illustrate a point, she touched his shoulder, like an old friend might. Or a lover. Or brother.

Haldane backed up, reversing blindly in the direction he had come, the curious glow slowly fading, until he felt it safe to turn and quicken his pace home.

The next morning Haldane went back to the same spot and found, stacked behind a tree stump, the devices that must have created the light. Mobile phones. About ten of them. All old, different sizes, their brand names either scratched off or faded away. He pressed the on button on one and it lit up. But there was no signal. None of the rest had either, and in most the charge that lit them up was already low or exhausted. Lying beside them was what looked like a case, newer than any of the phones themselves though it seemed too big for them. Then he saw it had a connection plug. He tried each of the phones and the connector fitted neatly into one of their pinholes. On the other side the device had a clear plastic panel.

"Duban! Duban!" Haldane called as he ran towards the door of the great chamber. Duban met him just before he stepped inside. "I don't know how I'm going to do it. Maybe I won't be able to. But, at the very least, I have a source of power!"

"Come in. Tell me."

Sitting down at the table Haldane showed him the phones. "And this," he said triumphantly, "is a solar charger! Don't you see? The charger gets power from the sun, which we have no lack of, the phones themselves are useless as phones but their batteries work. Look, they light up! If I charge one or two of them up and find a way of connecting them to the radio, that might be enough to power it."

Duban threw back his head and laughed till Haldane thought he might injure himself. "Of course! Ma'ahaba has collected these dud appliances from our occasional guests. When they can no longer use them she likes the light they give off to brighten the garden in the evening. But we had no way – until now! – of recharging them. Where did you find this?"

Haldane, unsure of the politics of Ma'ahaba's meeting last night evaded the question. "Well we can charge them now. But let's not to be too hopeful. I have no idea if my idea will work. And even if it could I have even less notion of how to do it."

"Ah. I know where it came from. We had a visitor only last night. We did not think it safe for you to meet him. He told us he could not find a radio battery, that he was sorry. But his little gift to Ma'ahaba might very well save our skins!"

"Maybe. I'll do what I can. What else did your friend from outside say?"

The old man turned serious. "That there has been little fighting of late in the immediate vicinity. That our people are safe for the moment, as are we ourselves."

"And beyond the immediate vicinity?"

"So far as he is aware your base is still where it was, but communication with it is more difficult than ever."

"And the war? In general."

Duban bowed his head. "There are brigades moving up from the south, opposing tank squadrons from the plains. I think this is what he said. The news is muddled. Talk of schisms on one side or the other, or both. Our guest himself was unsure of the details. Breakaway groups and bandit armies confusing the theatre of battle."

Duban leant over the table towards Haldane. "You want to understand what is happening in the war? You never will, my son, until one side or the other claims victory, and it all starts again. For you soldiers it is necessary, I imagine, that you have news and that you believe it. For those of us caught up in it, all reports are contradictory. Reports of conflicts are always conflicting!" he squealed, delighted with his joke.

"I'll take this radio outside and dabble. You can say a prayer."

Duban looked at him. "I'm joking, Duban."

The old man laughed again. "Asking assistance of the Sacred oft-times does the trick."

"And you honestly expect an answer?"

"Perhaps it has already been answered? We may be saved by energy from the skies! Aha!"

"Stored by a device invented by man. But to be honest, your praying's probably going to be as effective as my cor-rie-fisted tinkering."

Haldane settled himself on the grass just beyond the French windows, a cup of cool cardamom tea at his side. He had brought with him all the pieces of wire and little tools he had together with the various pieces of the radio's workings that had come loose. Within an hour he felt he was making sense of how the battery, which he was sure was drained, connected to the radio itself. He placed the solar charger against the wall of the house where he thought the light and heat might be most concentrated. Then he lay back on the grass, still grainy from yesterday's dust, and let the boughs and leaves fan him. When he opened his eyes Ma'ahaba was approaching, presumably from her usual resting spot.

"Have you made it work? The radio?"

"Nowhere near. But I have an idea."

"Do you want to? Make it work."

"Of course."

"Then back to the war."

"Can't stay here forever."

"Why not? We do."

"You could come with me."

She laughed. "Me?"

"And Aliyyah. And Duban, if he wanted. All of you. Why stay here?"

"You seem quite comfortable here, Captain."

He thought about this for a moment. "True. But because, I suppose, I know I will be leaving."

"Like it's a holiday?"

"Something like that."

"I did some of your holidaying when I was in your part of the world. We went to a beach town. Swam, and danced, sang songs at midnight by the water's edge. I wonder when my next holiday will be."

"Then come with me. If I ever get out myself."

"I might just, soldier."

"Would they let you?"

She laughed again. "I don't suppose the General would be too pleased. Then again, he might accept my decision. Especially if it turned out to be well-timed. It's hard to believe we will always be safe here."

"And Duban?"

"He'd be lost without me. Without me and Aliyyah."

"One so wise, so easily lost?"

Haldane wanted to ask her about the soldier visitor last night, but feared she would think he had been spying.

"I wonder what it would be like to be a soldier," Ma'ahaba said. "Me, a soldier. Would I be told that I look tough and professional, especially when I'm carrying a gun? Even more so if I was wearing lipstick." She clapped her hands, pleased with herself, the way Duban liked to do. "Or I could be like the Egyptian goddess. Isis. Wasn't it she who gathered the parts of her murdered and mutilated son, flung all over the earth, and stitched him back together and breathed life into him? The warrior mother bringing life, not death. What do you think, Captain?"

"This Isis would be a handy person to have on the battlefield."

"Your radio seems to be in bits and pieces." Ma'ahaba had a habit of changing the subject abruptly. He explained to her how he needed to find a way to connect it with the phone batteries.

"My fairy lights! We used to do that in university, turn our cells on when sitting on the lawn. And wave them, at concerts? Do they still do that? And now we have a way now of bringing them back to life again. And you think it could work for the radio? How clever you are."

"Yes, well, we'll see."

That day Aliyyah and Haldane spent, or so it seemed to him, less time together than usual. He had been busy all morning with the radio and she did not appear until late afternoon.

"Ma'ahaba has been helping me with my cerement."

"What's that?"

"A robe? But a special one we all have here. We make them ourselves, in preparation." Aliyyah giggled under her veil.

"Preparation for what?"

"For our wedding."

"Are you thinking of getting married, Aliyyah?"

"But the gown is not finished with then. We continue sewing, expanding it, embroidering."

"Why?"

"Eventually it will be the dress in which we meet our maker."

Haldane stopped walking. "It's a shroud? And a wedding dress? You spend all your life making your own shroud?"

"Hardly all my life. It's the first time in many days that I've taken it up. Ma'ahaba and I do both ours together. She is no better at it than I. We are butterfingers. But we tell each other stories. She tells me of her days out in the world. And I often just make stories up." She bent towards him, whispering a secret: "To be honest I think Ma'ahaba makes up her stories as well! But we don't care. It's fun."

In the evening as Haldane worked on the radio, Ma'ahaba and Duban came and went, the old man with a different book in his hand each time, she supplying the soldier with glasses of sweet fruit juices.

Haldane could see it must be possible to create a little series of phone batteries by connecting them to each other, but how many he might need to power the radio he had no idea. And anyway he had nothing to connect them with. He had tried the bits of copper wire Duban had given him, then bits of barbed wire from the fence, but they didn't work.

"I can't place them firmly in the jacks or whatever you call them. Perhaps that's the problem. Or maybe you need a special kind of wire."

"I may," Ma'ahaba said, "have a possible solution to the first problem. You place the wires in the little sockets and I'll bind them tightly with threads. Would that work?"

"Well, it's better than anything I've thought of. We could give it a try."

Haldane and Duban whiled away an hour in the library, supposedly looking for practical manuals but the old man getting distracted by rediscovered books, each of them it seemed printed in a different script. Eventually Ma'ahaba called them back to the table where she was ready with threads of every colour. Haldane set up three batteries in a row and poked the wires into the tiny holes. Ma'ahaba skillfully wrapped the corners of the batteries with threads, breaking off the ends with her teeth. Haldane then connected the jacks from the last battery and laid them over what he thought must be the right tiny pieces of metal. Ma'ahaba spun her delicate little web again. Then they switched on all the batteries and, finally, the radio. Depressingly, it remained dead.

"I have always believed that silence is eloquence," said Duban. "My confidence in the idea I admit is shaken, my friend."

Dispirited, Haldane decided to walk outside in the night air before retiring. The stars were fainter tonight and the darkness felt fuller than usual. And there was a different movement in the sky, sudden dartings, almost touching him. It took him a moment to realise they were bats, dancing darkly in the trees around him. Taking one of the little paths that led alongside the irrigation conduits he tried to think of solutions to the radio problem. Getting no inspiration he turned and made his way back to the house.

In the sky before him he saw an extraordinary sight. At first he thought his vision was playing up on him again, or that he was dreaming. But there, low in the night sky and some three hundred feet in front of him was Aliyyah, suspended in mid-air.

He could not see her features but it could only be Aliyyah – young, slight, slim, there was no one else in the house it could have been. She was dressed, as usual, all in white and the currents and zephyrs up there caught the material so that it willowed and rippled, her whole form ebbing and flowing unsupported.

Haldane quickened his step, alarmed for a moment that she was falling. But she remained where she was, looking out over his head towards the mountains behind, invisible in the dark. The fright the vision gave him, and the incomprehension at what he was witnessing, caused his heart to race and his head to thump. He felt, though he was the one safe on the ground, he was back in the helicopter being sucked out of the sky.

Approaching nearer to where she was drifting, he finally understood. Now he could make out the shape of the house, hidden in the night a few steps further back. The outline of the highest story of the house became clear, and he realised she was merely standing at an open window, lit

"But there, low in the night sky and some three hundred feet in front of him was Aliyyah, suspended in mid-air."

by lamplight in the room, the draft ruffling her gown. He laughed at his own stupidity and credulousness and, just when he was about to call up to her, she moved away from the window, closing it behind her.

Re-entering his own quarters the recon officer decided he had learned one thing at least from the experience: he was now quite certain where Aliyyah's bedroom was.

The Story of the Family Curse

he next morning, he was back staring at the radio, wondering what to do next, when Ma'ahaba entered. She stood watching him for a while then said, "You thought it might be the wrong kind of wire?"

"Or I'm connecting the wrong bits to the wrong bits. Or the wrong way round. Or the whole idea is misguided. Ma'ahaba I have no idea what I'm doing."

"But if it is a question of the wire. We have old lamps here. Perhaps the electrical cord in them might do the trick?"

"It's worth a try."

Together they went back to the great chamber and Haldane saw for the first time that there were old standard lamps, not unlike those he remembered from his childhood. They had wires and plugs that either lay useless on the floor, or were still plugged into dead sockets. After placing the charger back out in the sun, he used a knife Ma'ahaba brought from the kitchen to cut open the plastic covering on the cord. Inside were tendrils of wire similar to the copper stuff he already had but much finer, and different to the touch.

"One concern occurred to me last night," he said when Duban joined them. "Let's just say, and it's a long shot, that this works. I have no idea how much voltage or whatever the radio can take. Maybe we can't make nearly enough. Or worse, what if it works, and it's too strong and we blow that damned thing altogether?"

As they worried in silence together, Haldane looked at the old lamp. "Unless... Let's try this. I think there should still be enough power in some of those batteries for this little experiment."

When Duban had brought the batteries and Ma'ahaba more thread, they set up the sequence of batteries again and the soldier played around with the other ends inserting them into the bulb fitment. "How much of a shock can you get from a phone battery I wonder?"

None, as it turned out. And the bulb remained unlit. They tried connecting a second battery and, after endless configurations with the lamp end, Haldane felt a prickling on his skin. All three stared at the bulb and, gradually, the faintest of lights appeared.

"We have done it!" cried Duban. "Where there is unity, there is victory!"

"Well we've made a bulb glow. A bit."

With a third battery – and this time keeping it turned off until Haldane had stopped adjusting the bare wires – the lamp glowed perfectly bright. A fourth blew it entirely. Together they reckoned, purely through guesswork, that four might be about right to fire up a radio. Again Haldane tried different jacks and plugs and tiny slabs of metal in the motherboard, Ma'ahaba having to tie them on – a delicate operation, but which she managed each time with dexterity. And, just as the bulb had gradually come to life, so too did the radio set.

"Hallelujah," said Haldane, genuinely pleased with himself.

"Indeed, my friend. All praise belongs to God!"

"Except we've made it fizz and hiss," Haldane said, "but that's all."

"Be not afraid of progressing slowly, Thomas, only of standing still."

Haldane, playing with the dials and little antenna, shook his head. "Your optimism is admirable, Duban."

"Also," Ma'ahaba smiled, "often insufferable."

Haldane asked for a tray and set the radio, now in pieces clamped and stuck precariously together, on it. "I can take it back to my room and keep playing with it. Fingers crossed."

But back in his quarters, the radio made the same static white noise no matter how he adjusted the aerial or turned the buttons, and he suspected that the thing would never work. He conceded for the first time to himself that his unit might well have given up on him and he would never be able to make contact.

In all probability, he was numbered among the dead. He began to feel that, in a certain sense he was actually dead, or as good as. He was an echo of himself, reverberating in this dreamlike place, like the stagnant non-stop white noise of the broken transistor.

Memories of who he had once been were all he was left with and now those memories came back in quick succession, like a row of dominoes falling, each memory triggering the next. Mick the pilot – his name was Michael Samson, and he had been a friend since day one of Haldane's tour. That was eight months ago now, he reckoned. Or eight months from the day of the crash, whenever that was. Mick was brash and rowdy, forever making jokes, in the growling accent of his native city. No doubt it was something he had said that had made them laugh just before the 'copter bucked in mid-air. Gunner Simon was Simon Kane. Haldane remembered how he thought the two men had got mixed up: Mick, the working-class highly trained pilot; Simon the public schoolboy, finger on the trigger like an old-fashioned Tommy. The three of them got on well enough, as they had to, but there were arguments. Simon believed in the war, and saw the enemy as the enemy; Mick the professional swore that their leaders, military and political, were idiots. For his part, Haldane took an agnostic line, more to keep the peace between the three men than out of any considered position.

Now both comrades were dead. Their remains lying

out there in the lonely mountains of exile. As he was too. Marooned, sundered from his life, his world, in this inescapable no man's land.

And then Aliyyah comes to mind. Her green eyes like balm, her voice a liquid lullaby. She comes to him like medication, reviving him, and he knows that all is not lost. And yet. Renewed now, determined once more to keep fighting, he knows that his mission is to leave this place and most probably, Aliyyah, behind.

Curled up in his bed, limbs tight against his chest, under a single clammy sheet, the dreams that come to him do not feel like dreams, but all too real. The theatre of battle where he himself had acted. The burst of guns and the burst of blood. Howls and the sobbing of grown men, dying men, men without arms or legs, the stench of sodden darkness, the hopeless, endless, emptiness of it all. Amid the clamour he hears Duban's quiet voice: "Evil earns the evil it sows." Then Ma'ahaba's: "One life is not enough." And Aliyyah: "Death is our true home."

The sky was lit by an exploding shell and he saw his helicopter transformed, as it had been in other dreams, into a chariot pulling up and onwards, not down into the conflagration. He could see three bodies slumped inside – Mick and Simon and himself. But she who was driving it, he could not tell, in the spinning, the chaos, whether it was Ma'ahaba or Aliyyah.

After showering under the walled-off fountain, the water crisp from night, and washing off the shadows of his dreams, he placed the charger out in the sun and went back to sleep for a while. When he woke he considered the possible problems with the radio. It was bust completely – but not knowing for sure there were other things to consider. The antenna wasn't working. Or there was simply no signal here. He remembered vaguely that the armed forces used very high – or was it very low? – frequencies. Either way, wavelengths he did not have access to in this remote

"… and he saw his helicopter transformed … into a chariot,
pulling up and onwards, not down into the conflagration"

spot. Or perhaps he simply had to amplify whatever signal there might be.

He took the radio out into the garden, collected the refreshed charger and made his way down past the clearing where Ma'ahaba had met with her friend in the glow of phone fairy lights. From there further down the path to the back gate – the quickest way, as far as he could estimate, to the barbed wire fence. With the radio, batteries and charger all on an old tray from the dining room, the parts held well enough together. He placed the aerial against a metal pole in the fence and turned the radio on.

The hisses and fizzes began to change, first softening, then shrieking, until something resembling human voices and words began to emerge from the crippled machine. Men speaking, then a woman somewhere singing. More speech and crackles and back to the white noise. So now he could pick up something from the outside world. But how on earth would he be able to make contact with a tiny, covert military base amidst all the sounds and broadcasts of the planet? He had to hope that, by pressing buttons and twirling dials, throwing switches – there were so many controls on it – he would eventually find the right frequency.

That was a problem that would need to wait. He needed to walk, and he needed to speak with Aliyyah.

He found her sitting reading by the fountain held up by little lions.

"What's the book?"

"Oh old stories I first read as a child. I like to go back to them."

"What's the story you're reading now?"

"About two brothers, during a time of peace. Shall I tell you it?"

She seemed so eager, he did not want to disenchant her. She put down the book and turned fully towards him.

"The father of these brothers left them each land on either side of a mountain. The elder's land was blessed with sun most hours of the day, while the younger's lay mostly in shade. As a result, one farm was fertile and prospered and the other rocky and dry, its crops withering." Haldane got the impression that she was not so much recounting the story but reciting it from memory.

"The elder brother felt this to be unfair and decided to help make the dying land live again. But he did not want praise or thanks so he went about the task at night. For weeks he dug irrigation channels, sowing his own best seeds and grafting cuttings from his sturdiest crops. Eventually the shaded land began to bear fruit. He also, inch by inch, extended his brother's land into his own where it would be touched by the sun."

The soldier smiled at the girl's pleasure in telling the story, animated and wide-eyed.

"But the younger brother comes across him one night when the older was hard at work." And here Aliyyah frowned, almost comically. "Without asking, he realises what has been happening and the reason behind his recent good fortune. He approaches his brother, does not find the words, so simply embraces him. At once the entire mountain was lit up by the depth of their love, and the sky began to glow. And so, at night, when you see a light on the horizon, you know that, somewhere, brotherly love is blossoming."

"It's a very pretty story."

"Do you like it Tom? It's just a child's story."

"If only it were true."

"It is, in a way."

"Aliyyah." Haldane sat down beside her. "It is at least possible now that I will be able to inform someone out there of my whereabouts."

"I have heard that you have made progress."

"Even if I do manage to make contact, of course, rescue might still be impossible."

"You feel you need to be rescued, Tom?" Aliyyah said sadly.

"I only know it is my duty."

"But are you still a soldier? Even here?"

"I'd have thought you, Aliyyah, of all people would accept that duty is important."

"Why?"

"You seem… dutiful. You obey the laws of this house."

"Whilst I am here. And you, you obey them too. You are very respectful."

"Aliyyah. Would you consider leaving?"

She looked away and said nothing for several minutes.

"I will be sad. Sadder, I think, than perhaps I have learned how to be, when you leave."

He thought then she might get up and leave. But she picked up her book, and looked for a particular passage. When she'd found it she read out loud, though what meaning she intended for him, if any, in the story she chose, he could not tell.

"'Once, there was a princess, the Protectress, a custodian of the gates of Paradise, we may glimpse her nightly, in her chariot, a star shooting across the heavens.'"

He was thinking of her stories later that night as he sat down to dine with Ma'ahaba. He asked again, "Why does Aliyyah never eat with us?" But before she could answer Duban appeared at the door, looking troubled.

"Thomas. Will you come with me? There is something I need to show to you."

Haldane left his food untouched and followed as the old man bustled out into the hallway. He followed several steps behind until they arrived at the steps that led up to his room.

"You have passed these portraits on the wall several times every day since you came to us. Have you ever wondered about them?"

"I've noticed them."

"And what exactly have you noticed about them?"

"The men must all be related, though it's clear they lived at different times. Your family I assume?"

"Yes. Anything more?"

"I'm no expert but I think the artists weren't very good."

"On the contrary the portraits are splendid! Perfect."

"I know nothing about painting but they look to me as though they're painted by the same hand. But that can't possibly be the case. Unless, I wondered, if they were done by the one man, based on photographs or earlier portraits?"

"The similarity. Well done. In almost every detail. But look closer and you will see the brushstrokes are different. The canvases too. And the age of the paint. No, they were each created in their own time with the subject sitting before them, by different painters. Over a century of portraits and yet it is almost as if the same man has been painted over and over by the same hand."

"I wonder if all these official portraits are the same everywhere. I've seen the likes of them in barracks and headquarters and fancy buildings all over the world."

But Duban wasn't listening. He crooked his finger. "Come. Follow."

Duban retraced his steps, down the corridor that led eventually back towards the dining room, past the library, then opened a door that Haldane had not noted before. It led into another narrow corridor and the soldier knew that this must be the passage that connected the newer part of the buildings to the older. Indeed a few paces more and they arrived at the bottom of the grand staircase that Haldane had climbed following the sound of Aliyyah's voice.

As they ascended they stopped momentarily at each portrait, Duban not needing to say anything to drive his point home – the paintings here felt like more copies, excepting little details of dress and background, of those they had been talking about a moment ago.

At the top of the stairs, Duban said: "You think the artist is not good because he has failed to capture the spirit of the man, the life. That they are somehow dead in the frame. Dead before their time. But how can so many artists over so many decades share the same deficiency in their craft? The answer can only be because they did not fail. They captured each of these men perfectly. My family, Thomas, suffer from an affliction. And have for generations immemorial. Look harder at this last one," Duban pointed to a picture before them in the upper hall. "His eyes, like the rest, are dull, and lifeless. But not dead. See how he stares back at us, blank and brutal. There's a cruelty… No, that is not the right word. Vacuums, his eyes are vacuums. Cold. Heartless. Indifferent. Violently indifferent."

Whether it was under the spell of the old man's passion, Haldane could see what he meant. The man in the portrait did truly appear fearsome now. Though in all honesty the thought had not occurred to him before.

"All these portraits were made after my kinsmen had left this house and gone out into the world. While they were here, when they were younger men, they were, by all accounts, optimistic and cheerful. And they were all different, had their own ways of being, of speaking, their own enthusiasms. Eventually, as you see, they all became the same. Empty."

"I don't see how –"

"Whilst they were young and safe in this house, and close to our ancient laws and devotions, they were complete. But this is a military family. The moment they left, as it was their duty and their fate so to do, it was to fight wars. And each of them succumbed, quickly, to cynicism and indifference. Succumbed to the world."

"Duban, everyone knows that war is a vile thing. But not all soldiers lose their souls."

"It is you who use the word, not I. Come!"

Off he scurried again, and Haldane followed, feeling irritation rise in his breast. Another door opened to a room the same size and proportions as the great chamber downstairs. But here there were no lamps or carved cabinets, rugs or embroideries, none of the colour and warmth of the corresponding room below. This room was practically empty, save for a series of framed pictures on each of the four walls.

Approaching the nearest one, Haldane saw that it was not a painting but a photograph. A street scene. All women, some of them covered, others not. A pleasant, almost joyful snapshot of what looked like a perfectly ordinary day in a town somewhere, presumably not far from here. He moved to the next photograph and it was not dissimilar. This time it was a city and there were men and women going about their business. Again, lively and likeable but not depicting, as far as Haldane could see, any particular event. Just life. There were several more in the same vein, snapshots of normality. They had a nostalgic effect on the soldier, making him long for noise and bustle and people and movement. The photographs, in contrast to the portraits, marked time and the passing of years: from what Haldane thought might be daguerreotypes through black and white to digital images. In the earliest ones there were no motor vehicles, while in the most recent the roads were hectic with cars and buses. Fashions changed, particularly among the women, and in shop signs and cafes. And yet. There was something frozen about all the images. Despite all the changes and commotion they felt lifeless. As though the photographers lacked the same skills as the artists: the skill to animate the image. These visual records looked like fictions.

Duban touched his shoulder. "Look closer." The old man took him by the arm back to the first. He waited a moment then pointed to the top corner. There, almost indistinct, was a woman walking away from the scene, her back to us. "See how her head hangs low, her shoulders hunched?" All Haldane could see was a woman walking away, and if her shoulders were slumped it was probably due to the bag of messages she was carrying. At the next street scene Duban pointed out another women. This time nearer the front but to one side. Her hair was covered and she was veiled, revealing only the eyes. "But look at her eyes, Thomas! How bitter she looks. Don't you see?"

"I suppose. But she might just as well be surprised by the photographer, or thinking about something else."

"She is looking right at the photographer. At us, and she is pained."

At each photo Duban pointed out another woman. Each one of them alone, detached from the people around her and either turning her back on the camera, or like the second woman, staring at it. Duban always chose one of the older women, sometimes in a group surrounded by younger ones, laughing or chatting.

"We know these women, Thomas. They are of this house. I can name each of them."

"Even the woman in the distance with her back turned towards us?"

"You know so little about us, my dear friend, and there is not nearly enough time to explain. So I ask you to have faith in me, in what I know. When the men of this family go out into the world they become dogs of war. When the women leave they decline, they age before their time and they encounter only odium and disillusion."

Haldane looked quickly at each of the pictures in turn, then stepped back from Duban. "Sir. You've been very kind to me. You probably even saved my life. And I have, until now, found your conversation interesting, sometimes wise. But now I know what I've suspected. You are, Duban, quite mad." The soldier strode towards the door.

"At least I hope this is lunacy talking and not something more calculated."

Running down the stairs he heard Duban calling weakly after him. "Thomas. I beg of you. Do not take Aliyyah away from this house. You do not know what you do."

Haldane returned to the dining room where Ma'ahaba still sat, an untouched plate of food before her while she worked on an embroidery.

"Is that why you stay here?!" Ma'ahaba raised her eyebrows at Haldane's question, almost shouted at her. "Because of that old wives' tale?"

Ma'ahaba smiled. "That we all become monsters and strumpets if we leave this place? Who knows – perhaps it's true."

"It's ridiculous. You mustn't let him peddle that nonsense."

"Perhaps we all go to the dogs when we leave our homes. Old Duban might have a point."

Duban himself entered just as she said it. Haldane had never seen the old man so ill-tempered before. The eyes that usually radiated goodwill now glowered and his lips were taut. But his voice was calm.

"It is more than that. You know it is. I have no doubt that most of us poor mortals are cursed one way or another, but this house has its own particular blemish and has had for generations."

"Don't listen to him, Ma'ahaba."

"You're giving me instructions now, Captain?" Ma'ahaba, amused, returned his stare. "From what I hear of your nocturnal ramblings, I wonder if your father – or for that matter, your mother, whom you never mention – might not say that you share the curse of this house?"

Haldane laughed dourly. "Oh is that all you mean? That we grow up and become different from our parents' expectations? In that case, Duban, you are quite right. No child should ever leave his house."

"I cannot speak of others. I only know our circumstances here." The burn of irritation was dying in his eyes. "Let us talk no more of this. I simply ask you, as a friend and a guest – leave Aliyyah alone."

With that he exited, closing the door carefully behind him. Ma'ahaba returned to her embroidery.

The soldier saw that there was a bottle of wine on the table, already open, and one glass beside it. He poured, half filling the glass, and sat at the table. The wine tasted strong on his lips. Nothing like the soothing wine he had had at his first meal. This wine was earthy, meatier. He closed his eyes.

"Turn the other cheek."

He heard his father's words as clearly as he had heard Duban speak a moment before, and had to squeeze his eyes tight shut to keep himself from looking around. They were the words his father had said when he'd told him of his decision to join the army. Parent and child, both men now, had argued long and bitterly.

"So we turn our cheeks and pay others to protect us? Wasn't it the son of your God who went out into the world?" Haldane grimaced at the memory of his brittle fury. "You seem quite keen on disobedient sons. Isn't the lesson that we should go out into the world, not hide away in a country manse mouthing pieties?"

Haldane tried to stop the memory flooding through him, but could not. "Hell is here," he told his father. "Heaven is here – in the world." Where was his own father's under-standing and forgiveness! "You know what I think? If there really was such a being as your God then logically he'd redeem the Devil himself." Storming out, never to talk to his father properly again, he barked, "He wouldn't resurrect the dead, he'd revive the living!"

At last Haldane managed to shake himself out of the memory and the same old argument spinning around relentlessly in his head.

"Please tell me, Ma'ahaba, you do not believe this rubbish about curses?"

She kept her eyes on her embroidery for a moment or two before speaking. "I don't know. I have lived happily beyond this house, but then I am not, strictly speaking of this lineage," she sighed. "Curses and blessings. I am never sure that we little mortals are worthy of such great things. Like heaven and hell – they seem… out of proportion to me. Our puny exploits on Earth hardly deserve so much, don't you think, Captain?"

When he didn't answer, she went back to her needlework. "But I believe in dreams."

"These aren't dreams, Ma'ahaba. They're crazy theories and he makes everything he sees fit them!"

"I like to make things, Captain. Like this here. Each time I start on a new piece I want it to be what I see in my mind's eye. In my dreams."

Haldane was up out of his seat, pacing. "Of course it never happens," she continued. "It's not just that it's not as good as I had hoped, it's also different. Something other than what I had set out to make. There's a kind of destruction in everything we try to create. But that shouldn't keep us from the attempt."

"I'm sorry. I'm not quite following. I should sit. Calm down." And Haldane sat again at the table but could not stop his right foot from tapping the floor while his injured left ached.

"It doesn't matter. I'm only saying dreams make you do things that will never be what you dreamt. But we need to do something with them. Otherwise they may stop visiting us. And that would be death."

The night before the crash they had been talking and drinking, Simon Kane, Michael Samson and Thomas Haldane. The Thunder Boys they called themselves. But soon their banter had turned to argument. The morning of the reconnaissance mission, however, like the good soldiers they were, all disputes and insults had been forgotten.

It was a fine morning, and as Michael propelled them up off the ground their spirits were as airy as the vast bright sky. They were to penetrate new territory, valleys behind the northern mountain range. A simple check. There had been no reports of insurgents there. It was simply a belt and braces job, checking out the lie of the land. Even if they were to spot enemy presence their job was not to fight, but to bring home the data, chart positions, estimate numbers of men and guns, turn around, come home. Simon the gunner was there only as a precaution.

Tom Haldane, the youngest of the three, being the recon man, was leader of the mission. All went well until dipping over the sheer face of a highland crag, whooping as they roller-coasted down, Haldane spotted a lone figure.

What could he be doing there? The man was just walking – until he was startled by the sound then the sight of the helicopter above him. He was as astonished as they were. He must be, Haldane figured, thirty or more miles from any settlement or water source. Where was he going? They had identified no camps, no guerrilla base, no village. So far as they could see, several hundred feet above him, he was unarmed. Unburdened in any way.

Mick Samson turned his gun in the lone man's direction and made the noises of it firing, like a child playing. Simon Kane told him to stop it. Samson upped the ante and said he was going to fire for real. He swivelled the MC60 and put his eye to the front sight. Simon Kane, sitting in front of him, pushed back and flailed an arm out to knock him off balance. "I'm not going to kill the fucker!" Samson yelled, "Just scare him spitless."

Haldane couldn't sleep. He sat at the radio, running through stations, changing wavelength bands trying to find Extremely Low Frequency. But he wasn't really concentrating on it, instead letting the memory of that morning

"… until dipping over the sheer face of a highland crag,
whooping as they roller-coasted down, Haldane spotted a lone figure."

fill his mind. But it stopped there. Mick and Simon yelling at each other, arms thrashing. Then that sound. Small and inconsequential. Had Simon fired? Then the grinding noise. Then the spinning, like the helicopter had gone cockeyed, the cabin rotating and the rotor blades static. Then the feeling of being grabbed and pulled out of the sky. Then the blackness. Though this time, as he relived the plunge, there was a moment of light. The frenzied rocking of the machine must have tilted him in such a way that he caught sunlight, and he saw they were plummeting down, directly towards the man on the ground, still frozen in awe.

He walked away from the radio, still humming to itself in the dark, and stood by the window. He could just see the outline of the fruit on the tree, its redness stolen by night. Had he read somewhere that colours do not exist? They're a trick of the light. We make them up in our heads. That red fruit was not red at all, it was no-colour.

The man below them. It could only have been the man that saved his life. Was he also the same man who was talking happily in the campfire light and laughing with Ma'ahaba?

He did not go down for breakfast the next day nor did he seek out Aliyyah. He stood by his post, determined to make contact with his base, with his old, his true, life. Being in this house was driving him mad. The memories, the nightmares, the heat and the silence. Then there was the pain that extended from the back of his head down into his left leg. He should get that seen to soon, by a proper doctor. But that pain was nothing compared to the agony of not being with Aliyyah. Even when he was with her she caused him a kind of aching. The welcome pain you get when you swill alcohol around a toothache. Her absence was original pain.

As the day wore on, he read from cover to cover the old radio books that Duban had given him. He took them out to where he had now stationed the radio permanently, beside the fence. There, the charger could direct the solar energy directly into the batteries. He had tried so many configurations already, but he was sure he was making some headway, keeping a mental note of those combinations that either lost signal entirely or tuned him in to what sounded like normal FM or medium wave, albeit very distant stations. There were only so many possible combinations. He spent hours now, and found that a combination of a channel 9 setting, tuned to 57.975 MHz, placing the aerial so that as much of the length of it as possible touched the metal stake, and switching to an S/RF setting, the white noise changed – and changed to a tone, a pitch, that he recognised. Underneath it there were voices. Intermittent, barely audible. Only the odd word discernible. But words in his own language. Not an announcer, but conversation, an exchange of messages, communiqués. If there was some kind of encryption – which had worried him – he had either accidentally unencrypted it, or the setting had remained since the morning of the crash. Whatever, he was convinced he was connected to, if not his own base, then a British Army presence somewhere in the region.

There was still one unknown factor. The radio had its microphone built in. It didn't look as if it had been damaged. But, though Haldane knew he could now hear his comrades, would they be able to hear him? He switched the apparatus off and stared at it for some time, before getting up and leaving his room deciding, for the time being, to keep his breakthrough secret.

Haldane stepped out into conditions he had not experienced here before. There were no stars and the darkness felt more than just night. More surprising still was the humidity. Since he had arrived the heat, under sun or moon, had been dry. But now there was warm moisture in the air and his skin prickled and sweat budded under his hairline. A welcome change that somehow seemed connected to being in contact with the outside world. He walked round to the back of the house and found the window where he had seen Aliyyah floating in mid-air. A lamp was lit within.

"Aliyyah," he whispered and almost immediately her silhouette loomed at the casement. When, almost as quickly, she was beside him and they stepped together towards the orchard he felt, in the darkness, that it was her shadow he was walking with. Aliyyah guided him towards the fountain of little lions as though it were midday. There, they talked as they always did, little or no pattern or logic to their conversation. Memories and observations, lines of poems and sudden thoughts, flowing as fast and smooth as the stream by their feet.

Then she took his hand for the first time. Shadow hand on shadow hand, shadow figures intertwining. He could barely see what she had done, but her cool palm, her gentle touch was both encouraging and distressing. The delicacy of her. Hold her too tightly and he feared she might break, too loosely and she may draw back.

He kept to his decision not to tell her directly of his progress with the radio, but said instead: "Tomorrow, or soon, I will be on my way from here."

"That was always so," she said quietly.

"It's best for you that I go. For everyone."

"It sounds, Tom, that you have made a decision."

Haldane wasn't convinced he had made any decisions. Events, and duty, and the will of others were shaping his actions. They sat in silence for a long time until they were walking again, slowly, ambling, the soldier like a blind man being led. The darkness began to thin out. No single part of the sky brightened but dawn was approaching, wrinkling the air. Somewhere far off, Haldane thought he could hear singing. Not from the house, and not the voice of either Duban or Ma'ahaba. A low hum, a single voice, male, chanting, as though the coming day was announcing its own arrival. The music was foreign to Haldane yet it reminded him of home, of a sung call waiting for a response.

At the house soldier and girl parted company. In the now pearl-grey light he could make out her features, but only just, like she were a ghost and her sad smile wishful thinking.

"I will tell you when."

She nodded and turned, disappearing, in her white robe and shawl, into the mist of daybreak.

Haldane made his way to the door of the great chamber, and was surprised to see Ma'ahaba there, reading what looked like letters by the window in the soft light.

"Has the bugle called already?" she asked.

"Excuse me?"

"Reveille. Soldiers rise early. All systems go."

There was water on the table but Haldane, refreshed now by the cool morning, decided not to drink. He sat across from her and stretched.

"I think I might be able to contact my unit soon."

"Well done, soldier. And what will you say? 'Mayday, Mayday.' Or is that not said anymore?"

"If I manage to get them to hear me, I'm not sure how I'll describe where I am."

"They'll find you. Once they know you're alive."

"And you can finally get rid of me."

"Captain, believe me, you have been a most pleasant distraction."

"I could ask, if they come and get me, for a Puma. Big enough to rescue all of us."

Ma'ahaba laughed, "Aliyyah told me you feel you need to be rescued."

"They could take a number of people. If any of your allies, out there, are in danger…"

93

"I think such a plan would put them in more danger, not less."

"If Aliyyah decided to come with me, would you try to stop her, Ma'ahaba?"

"Have you asked her?"

"I'm not sure I should, if you set yourself against it."

"You overestimate my power, Captain."

"Would Duban?"

"Of course."

Then she went back to her reading. Haldane sat for a moment longer deciding he should get some rest, shower in the fountain, freshen up for the moment when he'd try to speak to his superiors. As he was getting up Ma'ahaba held up the page in her hand. Haldane could see it was written, in a script he didn't know, by hand.

"Did you know, Captain, that some very clever people think that, mathematically, a single universe is impossible? We are, if I understand it right, in just one of many multiverses. I like the word! It sounds like a long song, perhaps a ballad. And if the very clever people are correct it doesn't really matter what you – or I, or Aliyyah, or Duban – decide to do. If you go alone in this world, in another world, very like this one, one or more of us goes with you."

"That's ridiculous."

"I think it's a wonderful idea. Comforting, don't you think? In another world, every bit as real as this one, you died in that accident. And there is no war. And I am not here but in Cambridge, and Aliyyah is with her mother and father at court."

Haldane got up wearily. "I'm not going to pretend to understand what you're talking about." But at the door he stopped and smiled. "Though my bet is, in every one of those worlds, there is a Duban, guarding the gate."

He lay naked on his bed, the heat of the day intense and broiling his dreams. Not fully asleep he tried to stem, ashamed, visions of Aliyyah in his arms, kissing him, her body revealing itself to him in glimpses through the folds and pleats of her robes, her skin touching his, her lips exploring him. But falling into real sleep the visions took over and entangled themselves with those other memories and apparitions that had haunted him nightly. Aliyyah's sighs became the sound of the dying engine. Her warm lips mouthing the gunner's words: "Scare them spitless." As their bodies merged they seemed to fall together, floating down, rocking, hot. The dream of Aliyyah became like a dream within the dream, fading in the uproar, her body desiccating in the heat, her cries ever more distant.

Every so often he would jolt awake with a shout but the heat and the fierce light from the window sent him back quickly into his dreams again. And soon the shadow of Aliyyah came back, and in force, changing, in fits and starts, into another form. Until in his arms was not her at all but Ma'ahaba, in the younger girl's clothes, throwing her head back, laughing as she'd done with the unknown soldier in the campfire. The bigger, bustier woman, was stronger, heartier and more direct in her lovemaking, grappling with him and holding his eye, her confidence outgunning his. Still they were plunging and as they spiralled down, wheeling in the air, bumping back up every so often as if caught in a pocket of turbulence, Ma'ahaba's laughter turned from joy to defiance and finally something almost like malice, wild eyes glaring at him as though he were to blame for their fall. When she spoke it was with Duban's voice: "You take nothing from this house!" Behind her he saw Aliyyah, slumped in the gunner's seat, and he knew she was dead even when she lifted her bloodied head and spoke, in his father's voice: "The dead will not be resurrected."

Finally awake, the horrors silenced, Haldane lay sweating and weeping in the unforgiving heat of the sun.

Later, leaning against the barbed wire of the fence, he felt wearied and discouraged. Over and over again he tried speaking into the radio microphone, adjusting the one control it had. He gave up on his formal tone and what he thought might be correct protocol, resorting to hellos and "Can anybody hear me?" He might have drowsed for a while, and thought at first he was dreaming, but he heard a voice that seemed to be addressing him directly.

"Unknown station. Verify." The radio operator was clear if faint.

"Captain Thomas Haldane. RRS. 274000."

"Break-Break. Come, in Captain. Your position? Ready to copy."

It was all so simple, so formal. As if they had been expecting his call. Exactly what more was said he couldn't remember even moments later. All he knew was that the deed was done. Connection had been made. They knew who, and where, he was. And that he'd better smarten up quickly now. The communication over, Haldane stared out through the wire to the distant mountains. They stared back at him as blankly as ever but everything had changed. Somewhere beyond those arrogant hills, tanks were rolling, their turrets turning, surface-to-air missiles wheeled into position, knives sharpened, visors lowered. Captain Haldane's world was about to storm into life.

He'd imagined Duban would have been happier about the news. The old man listened and nodded his head.

"Do you think they understood where you are, Thomas?"

"On the second call they seemed to have worked it out. Though I'll have no way of knowing until they get here. If they get here."

"And when might that be, my friend?"

"Tomorrow night."

"So soon? And at night?"

"Security I imagine. A covert mission, not least to protect the whereabouts of your house from the enemy."

"Ah. The enemy," and Duban's brow furrowed. "A pity it is to be so soon."

"And here I was thinking you couldn't get rid of me quick enough, Duban."

"A paradox, I agree," and for a moment the old man's face lit up again. "It is best you go, though none of us desires it. What the Pythagoreans called Dyad, I believe."

"You will be happy to spend more time with your books, instead of arguing with me, or changing my bandage!"

"So we should celebrate these last days together. Here, cardamom tea, let us drink the way we did that first morning. And let us talk all day and through the night!"

Haldane accepted the cup, and it tasted as reviving as ever.

"You once called me a teacher, Thomas, and though I denied it, I was flattered. Flattery is to be smelt not swallowed. The matter of understanding is so deep it is available only to those who already have it. I do not claim to be among them."

"Ah yes. I remember that argument. The gift of Faith. You can't get round that one. And it's not just you pious folk that use it. Guy in my unit got out of every political argument by saying that the rest of us had false consciousness."

Haldane lowered his eyes. "A shadow has passed over you, Thomas. Was he one of your comrades you lost in the accident?"

The soldier did not reply. Duban allowed a moment to pass, then said, "It is true. I have taught you so very little."

"Probably, I'm just a bad student."

"On the contrary you are an ideal one! Forever asking, then disputing!"

"And Aliyyah?"

"As a student? Precisely the same!"

"Duban. You do not really believe in this curse."

97

"Think of it, rather, as an affliction. Would that help you to understand? You believe in genetic disorders."

"I know there are sicknesses that are passed on from generation to generation. But I doubt there is a gene for depravity."

"It is possible."

"Is it? I don't know. But I'm not going to worry about it until someone discovers it."

"That is a dull answer, Thomas."

"We're back to looking for what isn't there. Doesn't it frustrate you, Duban, this going round in circles?"

The old man ignored the question. "You only believe in what you can touch, possess, and what your high priests tell you."

"Just as well I'm leaving."

"A shame. I am only beginning!" Duban laughed and broke the mood that threatened to sour between them. "But I ask you one last time. Consider it possible that an old man with too much time on his hands knows something that you do not. Here is a proposition. Desire makes slaves out of kings; patience makes kings out of slaves. When your men arrive, leave with them alone. You know where we are. Let Aliyyah consider, without pressure. Should she choose to join you, and preferably at a time when the war is abating, send for her."

"I am putting no pressure on her whatsoever, Duban. In fact I haven't broached the subject with her."

"Then please do not now."

"But I think returning is unlikely." Haldane got up and crossed the floor to sit next to the older man. "I want you and Ma'ahaba to come with me too. My unit will find a way of getting Ma'ahaba to General Deimos in the capital. From here she has no chance. All of you will be stuck, until the war draws closer. All of you need to leave!"

Duban looked hard at Haldane for several moments. "With you, Thomas, everything is one or the other.

Presence, absence. Leave, stay. Black and white. You see how little I have managed to teach you? You refuse to consider us. You have been here with us, but you have remained apart. Your soldierly discipline. You judge everything by what you can touch. You only know how to ask how, but are ill-equipped to ask why."

Upstairs he got ready. It didn't take long. With an old cloth he cleaned his boots as best he could. His uniform had not been worn since the day he first woke up here. And though he had tumbled out of a burning helicopter in it, it was perfectly presentable now. He kept running, to and fro, from his quarters to the radio by the fence, checking that the power and signal were still strong, that the whole rickety contraption was still working.

His leg felt better and he decided he should take off the bandage. He had never inspected the wound himself, had no idea even where the injury was let alone how bad. It took longer than he'd thought – Duban had a system of binding that seemed to leave no loose end. Eventually he had to cut and tear it off, using the little wire cutters.

He could see virtually no sign of damage. Redness on the back of his lower leg and knee, but that could have been caused by the bandage itself. Perhaps the injury was internal, a broken or fractured bone. Pacing his room, however, his leg felt fine, better than ever. And he realised that the ache in his neck had gone too. He smiled – good old Duban. He might talk in riddles but he clearly knew something about nursing. The soldier felt firm and strong, vigorous for the first time since his arrival. He was ready for whatever the coming hours would bring.

He made his way to the clearing where Aliyyah was already waiting for him. The blurriness of his vision had gone and the trees and plants around him didn't flare as they had seemed to nor did the sun hurt his eyes. Aliyyah, too, looked different to him. She was very pretty, that was sure, but he saw as she sat, playing with a flower in her hand, that she was a simply dressed young woman, her hair roughly cut, and in her still bright-green eyes a nervousness. Haldane felt he was fully in this place now and could see and understand better. And he loved Aliyyah all the more for seeing the real, apprehensive woman she was. He took her hand and they set off for their fountain.

"Tomorrow evening, not long after sundown, a helicopter will be here. You know I'd like you to come with me. I'd like you all to come with me."

"Ma'ahaba will not go."

"You've discussed it?"

"I think she is very tempted, but she thinks it will end badly for her."

"The minute we get across the frontier, we will contact General Deimos, and arrange to fly her directly to him."

"I'm not sure she wants that. And if she left here and did not go to him… But, really, I think it's because she is content here. She likes arguing with Duban. She gets her letters. There is company every now and then when villagers pass by. She thinks perhaps it is best to sit out the war here rather than in an army camp, or the capital where we hear there is often trouble."

"Does she think that is best for you too?"

"Ma'ahaba gives me no advice. I must do what I think is best."

"She's right, Aliyyah."

"I haven't normally considered what is best just for me."

"Do you feel you would be deserting Ma'ahaba?"

"Ma'ahaba says I am young. It's what Duban says too – but by that he means I should stay."

"We're all giving you advice. I'm sorry. But I genuinely believe you should leave here. But please be clear, Aliyyah. It isn't just because I want to be with you. I do. More than I know how to say. But you will be a free woman when you leave, free to decide what you want to do. And whatever that is, I am certain it will be better than staying here. Until the war knocks on your gate, or the rebels are defeated. Or General Deimos loses power. Or Duban dies." Aliyyah flinched only at the last one. "I'm sorry. But I think you have to be logical about this, think through your options."

"I have done nothing but, for quite some time now. I'm not interested in your freedom – if I go with you it is for us to be together."

He put his arm around her waist. "Thank god for that," he laughed. "I couldn't bear to leave you. Not here, or anywhere else in the future. My commission is nearly up. If it's too long for you to wait, I'll find a way of getting out. We'll go travelling, in safe and beautiful places!"

"To the milky city you spoke of, with the books and the hills and the temples?"

"Did I mention temples?" he laughed.

Aliyyah sat up straight so that she was looking down on him and said, "I will go with you, Tom."

"We will go wherever you want, darling, and live how you want to live. Everything you do and love here – we'll find a way of bringing your life with us." They laid their heads back against the cool stone, closed their eyes, and daydreamed together.

"It is intriguing, Tom. You have so much trouble believing in something as unworldly as a god, but you act so doggedly in the name of something even more fanciful."

"And what is that?"

"Love."

As he went down to dinner that night, uniformed and shoes on his feet, there was a spring in his step that he wasn't sure he had felt before, not just here but in his whole life. His stay, he thought, had been a genuine convalescence. The long hours of sleep – though they had been disrupted by unwelcome dreams – the walks, sunshine, the meagre but healthy diet. He had lost weight, felt rested, and now he was taking a prize he had not known existed back to his own world.

His sense of celebration was made even greater when he saw, at the table, not only Duban and Ma'ahaba in their usual places, but Aliyyah too. Dressed in bright embroidery – the work, he knew now of Ma'ahaba's hand – she sat and smiled broadly at him when he entered.

Duban was less pleased and Ma'ahaba looked lost in thought, barely greeting him. But they dined together peacefully enough. There was wine on the table. A bottle, Haldane thought, that was similar to the special, and supposedly last, one they had had before. But none of them took it – Haldane because he wanted to preserve the feeling of clarity he was enjoying.

They ate first small dishes of artichoke and mint with a red sauce that Haldane thought might be made from pomegranate. His sense of taste was as sharp as he felt generally and the food tasted bright and energizing. No mention was made of any plans for the following night until, as Duban got up to fetch the next course, Haldane decided to speak plainly.

"I cannot give you an exact time, but soon after nightfall tomorrow my people will airlift anyone who wishes to go to safety."

"How sure of this safety are you, Captain?"

"Perfectly, Ma'ahaba. There's no doubt you will all be safer there than here. And wherever you decide to go afterwards." He turned to face the older woman directly. "If any of your allies or friends wish to join us, there will be space for them, if you can let me know how many."

Duban re-entered with a tray of salvers. "Your planning is not quite so accomplished as you suggest, Thomas. You know very well our friends only visit us sporadically. We have not had time to forewarn them of your proposal." Under the lids of the silver platters were rice with nuts, aubergines, vine leaves with fillings that smelled of coriander and honey. "And may I say, my son, you use the term 'ally' somewhat loosely. I imagine we all do."

"I don't follow."

Ma'ahaba answered. "Factions within factions. Changing sides. Even our 'allies' are a little uncertain these days who is fighting whom."

"Let alone why," Duban added.

"Confused," Aliyyah said softly, as if to herself. "Confusion frightens me. Not understanding what is going on leads to fear. And fear leads to hate. Hatred to violence."

Duban considered her sorrowfully for a moment, then spoke to Haldane. "A decision taken thousands of miles away apparently alters everything these days. A slight turn in local loyalties… The man who saved you, Thomas. No one is quite sure if he's on the same side anymore."

"Not that he, or his friends, have changed sides," said Ma'ahaba, "but the sides around him may have."

"All wars begin simply enough," Duban sighed. "When war rages, the laws are dumb, and reason dies. Eventually old friends are sundered, brother fights brother, until battle erupts in every individual's heart. In all likelihood you, Thomas, will be safe, though even that cannot be assured. As for the rest of us…"

Haldane turned to Aliyyah. "Don't let them scare you. I will ensure your safety. Something I can't do while you remain here." He turned to the others. "Or you."

"I think Tom is right. Please come with us," the young woman spoke confidently. "So many things could go wrong here. Even if the war doesn't reach our door, our protectors may have to flee, and then we might starve."

Duban looked at the food, untouched, on his plate. "We shall not starve. We do not ask for much and what we need the earth supplies. It is our very remoteness, my child, that protects us. Few people know of us – though that," he shot a look at Haldane, "will change tomorrow night. Those who do know us, shield us. The General looks after us from afar. Out there, you will have only Captain Haldane. Captain Haldane who considers the idea of remaining among loved ones and praying for peace foolish activities."

"In my base camp they have services, Duban. Soldiers meet and pray with the chaplain. Across the line, the enemy are summoning their god. Hundreds of men dropping to their knees and screaming out to the heavens. If there are gods up there they're probably killing and mutilating each other too. The heavens are ablaze, and we fan the flames." Haldane shook his head. "It seems to me, sir, that prayers are more often offered up for victory and death than for peace. Those pious little words rising up from the earth like nerve gas. Yes, sir, with the greatest respect those decisions are foolish."

"While you fire the guns. And out of faith, Thomas. Faith that you and your men can make us all like you and then we shall all be happier and better. But is it so?"

"Yes. It is. Aliyyah, for instance, can live a full life."

"I already do, Tom. And I did even before I met you. Now it is simply full in another way."

"Our friend," Duban spoke to Aliyyah, "thinks us backward. We have not given up the things he has. We have not seen the light he has seen."

Ma'ahaba put her hand on Duban's. "Come now uncle, the Captain is man of action and all men of action are dreamers at heart. I wonder, Captain, in my rustic way, what if in the future it is discovered that the human animal needs illusion? To survive. Including the delusion that we needn't be deluded?"

She stood up and began clearing the platters and salvers away though no one had eaten much. Haldane helped her. "May I tell you a silly story?" she said. "To pass the rest of the evening without more squabbles."

Nobody replied, so Ma'ahaba began, as she worked. "One day a poor man finds a lamp, lying unclaimed in the street. He takes it home, and begins to polish it. Nothing happens. The poor man says, 'How I wish I could believe in genies.' Upon which, a genie emerges! 'That,' says the genie," and here Ma'ahaba put on a deep voice, "'was your first wish. I grant you two more.' The poor man, not want-ing to be selfish but rather share his discovery with all man-kind says, 'I wish all men believed in genies. How much better their lives would be.' The genie snaps his fingers and says, 'It is so, if you wish it. And your final request?'"

Ma'ahaba sat back down to finish her tale. "The poor man thought long and hard and decided that he had been generous enough and should look after his own desires. 'I wish,' he said, 'for a beautiful jewellery box crammed full of sapphires and diamonds and emeralds and rubies!' The genie snapped his fingers again. But no such box appeared. 'What's wrong?' the man asked, and the genie replied, 'Just because you believe in me, doesn't necessarily mean I exist.'"

No one responded to her story. But after a moment, Aliyyah spoke. "I dreamt of you last night, Tom. You were walking up a hill. You looked weary, but like a man at the end of his journey, his mission accomplished. It was in a strange land. Or strange to me at least. A cool, creamy place. And the sound of the sea. Or how I think the sea might sound, having never heard it."

"Were you there, Aliyyah? Were you there with me?"

"I did not see myself. But I suppose I might have been. If I was the see-er." And she laughed at the idea. Then she stood and looked at Duban. "Master, you have taught me everything, and every moment was a joy. And every ounce will stay with me until the day I die. One of the many things you taught me was that those who do not move do not notice their chains. I have noticed them now. And I know it is right that I go with Tom tomorrow. I will walk up that hill by his side."

Duban closed his eyes. Aliyyah went to Ma'ahaba, and

embraced her. Aliyyah went to Ma'ahaba, and embraced her. "Am I doing the right thing?"

Ma'ahaba held on to her. "I do not know, Aliyyah." Then she loosened her embrace to look at her stepdaughter's face. And she smiled. "One of the very many things I do not know."

"Oh Ma'ahaba, I will not miss you because you will be with me every day. I know you cannot leave Duban here alone. But I pray in my heart that one day you will join us, and we can live through the stories you told me of the old days." She then crossed to stand at Haldane's side. She took his arm and led him towards the door.

Duban, his eyes still closed, said, "It is a mistake, Aliyyah. My powers weren't enough to keep you here. But you will know. You will come to see that I was right. I am done with words. I have failed them. We must now witness what awaits us all when language ends."

In the doorway Aliyyah turned and, to the soldier's surprise, she laughed. She looked at her uncle, shook her head, and laughed. Haldane laughed with her, as the old man bowed his head.

Throughout the next day Haldane felt as strong as ever, but he was anxious. He made contact twice more with his unit to make sure that all parties were agreed on the plan and that nothing was going wrong. In the early morning he met only briefly with Aliyyah. She wondered what she should take with her.

"Nothing, my dear. It will make the rescue easier if we're not carrying anything."

"Oh but my robe. I haven't finished it yet."

"You mean the one that becomes your shroud – leave that of all things!" Haldane laughed.

"It is also a wedding gown."

"We'll find you something much better."

He noticed that the cape and shawl she was wearing

were old-looking and grey, presumably keeping clean clothes for the flight to safety. She spoke about other items she had wanted to take with her, some books and embroideries, but she began listing them in her own tongue.

"When we get out of here, you must teach me your language."

"I'm sorry. Was I not speaking English?" She looked worried for a moment. "Forgive me. I'm tired." They turned and made their way back to the house. Haldane could see she was nervous, strained. As she must be, taking the biggest decision of her life.

He did not seek her out for the rest of the day, much as he wanted to encourage her, he must have faith in her resolve. Once or twice he went down to the great chamber but never found anyone there. As always there was water and fruit and cardamom tea for him.

Sitting on his bed he had, for the first time, a clear picture of his mother in his head. A dainty woman, always smiling. "A saint," everyone said. His father, his teachers, parishioners. Her life, everyone agreed, was in the service of others. She was always helping some poor or sick neighbour, or at prayer meetings, or praying, cleaning the church, talking to believers and non-believers alike. In his mind's eye she was indeed smiling, radiantly, somewhere just above his head.

But then it came to him what had made her seem so withdrawn from him. When he was young, just a boy, she had become ill. He was too young to understand, but the illness was in her head, not her body. She forgot things, became confused, and he remembered vividly, painfully, the first time she forgot his name. He saw now she was not old at the time, but he knew even then that this should not be happening to her. What she never forgot, however, was her prayers. The last time he saw her, as he was leaving to go to war, she did not know how to say goodbye to him, but sat in her seat by the window, whispering the

Lord's Prayer. The soldier sat on his bed and wept, deeply and, he thought, for the first time, at the long slow separation from his mother. Until he decided he must stop. That weeping was pointless. Today of all days, when he needed to be strong and ready for the night's task. He stood to attention, back straight, forcing himself to be and look like the professional soldier he was.

He didn't hear a sound all day, as if everyone had left the house. Doubtless they were ensconced in their private rooms. Would Ma'ahaba come out tonight to bid them farewell? Was Duban somewhere devising ways of obstructing Aliyyah's departure? Might he try and lock Aliyyah in her room? Then Haldane thought that unworthy of the old man – Duban might have crazy notions and be overly protective but he would not harm his charge in any way, nor physically try to constrain her.

Dusk fell. And it felt like a protective layer, like cover fire, as if the first part of his plan had gone right. Slowly – too slowly – evening hardened into night. The soldier put on his uniform and his boots. He took the radio, and some tools, and went out for the last time.

He exited via the great chamber, turned at the near wall of the house, heading towards the old fountain where he had showered in the afternoon. Taking the path to the original front of the building where the door within a door lay between alabaster carvings, he saw that Aliyyah was already outside, and waiting. She was sitting, staring straight in front towards the gate. He spoke her name softly but she didn't hear. Only when he was almost next to her and spoke again did she react. She looked up at him and he knew she was frightened.

Tonight the moon was out and the stars clear. Aliyyah now, although she seemed to him pale in the moonlight and fragile, she was no shadow, but flesh and blood, his companion, perhaps one day soon his spouse, as real and as mortal as he. Her eyes cloudy olive in the night. They took each other's hands. "Ready?" he asked. She nodded and they set off down the path.

In his urgency to get to the appointed spot – the old gate – the path seemed longer than ever, winding pointlessly round copses of trees and bushes. He checked every few seconds that he had the pliers to cut the chains on the gate. Hopefully that wouldn't be necessary – the 'copter would hover this side of the wall and winch them both up without difficulty.

Halfway along Aliyyah turned to take an offshoot path.

"It's this way, Aliyyah, no?" The girl looked confused for a moment, then nodded, smiled hesitantly and took his hand to follow him. He felt her shiver, out of agitation surely for the night was warm and close.

They did not speak, Haldane straining, listening for the first hum of the aircraft. By what he reckoned to be two-thirds along the route there was still no sound. That was okay. They may have to wait a little for their rescuers. So long as they were in the right place at the right time, ready, they could wait all night.

At least there was no sign of Duban. Nor – and it disappointed him – of Ma'ahaba. Though it was possible, of course, that the old man would be waiting by the gate. Whenever the path was straight enough and free of roots and stones, he searched the skies. It was possible that the high-altitude airstream was running in such a way that they would see the 'copter before they heard it. The stars seemed lower, closer, tonight than ever before. Great splashes of silver, throbbing fretfully, as if the sky were trying to eject them.

Aliyyah tripped once or twice, though she knew this path so well and normally she was nimbler and surer-footed than he. When he caught her arm, at her third stumble, he felt how thin her arm was, the bone close under the skin.

At last he recognised the shape of the last twist in the path that took them out at the gate. At the same moment they heard a distant buzz that seemed to come from the stars themselves, droning like wasps. He could see, far off, but low, a red light flashing and knew that everything was on schedule. Turning the final bend he thought the gate was clear.

A moment later, Duban stepped out into the clearing.

"One last time, do not leave us, Aliyyah. I shall not speak again. No words of mine will influence either of you. But I will remain here. My presence is not a reproach, merely a reminder."

Haldane could tell by the sound that the helicopter was large, probably a Puma, and it was approaching faster than he had anticipated. "Stand back, Duban. We need space." But the old man placed himself directly in front of the gate, in the middle of the clearing, where it would be easiest for them to be picked up.

Haldane took the radio and placed it on the ground, switching it on so that it lit up in the dark. It didn't give much of a glow but, apart from a few lanterns in the house some distance away, it was the only light in the vicinity. He knew that the instruments on the aircraft would find them anyway, picking up the radio waves, and with the powerful searchlights that were already sweeping the sky.

"Move away, man!"

But Duban stood his ground. Soon the massive Puma was over his shoulder and heading directly for them. Haldane clenched Aliyyah's hand tight. "Don't worry. They'll let down a ladder. Your uncle will be fine." He had to shout now over the noise of the engine. "You will go first. I'll help you climb up!"

"Aliyyah!" Ma'ahaba's voice was distant and high as she rounded the bend towards them. She was half-running, but stopped short of them. "I'll stay here. I only wanted to say goodbye."

Aliyyah turned to her and Haldane could feel her hand tremble, and the blood in her wrist pound. "Please, Ma'ahaba, come with us!" He shouted. The older woman shook her head and remained where she was. Haldane looked to Aliyyah, expecting her to make a final plea to her oldest friend. But she did not. She merely stared in Ma'ahaba's direction as though there was nobody there at all.

With the helicopter now nearly over them, Ma'ahaba screamed at the top of her voice to Duban. "Get out of the way! Let them go, Duban!" But he, too, remained motionless, looking up at the helicopter, so near it blocked out moon and stars, and seemed larger than it really was, looming in the dark. It dropped down further still and a soldier could be seen lowering the ladder. As it dropped, closer and closer, thundering, the more it swayed under the turbulence of its own blades. Haldane pointed to the radio on the ground, and shouted towards Ma'ahaba. "It still works! We can speak. Whenever you wish." He couldn't tell if she had heard or not.

The ladder was near enough now for Haldane to jump up and catch hold of the end of it. His comrade, not far above, gave instructions through the loudspeaker. "One at a time, until each of you is halfway. Women first, then the men. You last, Captain."

Haldane pulled the leather and steel ladder over and placed the end so that it was just a step up for Aliyyah. But she seemed frozen to the spot. He had to lift her up, upon which she did put her foot on the lowest rung, but made no attempt to climb further. "Come on, Aliyyah. It's perfectly safe. A couple of steps. I've got you. The soldier will take your arm in a moment." The 'copter suddenly lurched and the ladder swung out. Aliyyah made no sound but he could see her stiffen. He managed to hang on to her. Then she turned and looked down on him and for an instant, the draft blowing her robe and veil and hair wildly, she seemed to him dead. Her eyes were open, staring at him, but as if she were seeing nothing. So frail and motionless, hanging in the sky, the moonlight turned her skin yellow and ancient, the green gone from her eyes, only the whites showing. Haldane almost cried out but he controlled himself, and decided it best that he get ahead of her on the ladder and pull her up rather than pushing from below.

Just as he was level with her he saw a shadow rushing towards them from the ground. Duban. Screaming some words in his own language, he grabbed the girl's ankle so that he and Haldane were hauling in different directions. "Let go you stupid old bastard!" But Duban put his arms round Aliyyah's legs and hung on tight.

"Captain. What the hell's happening here?!" The soldier above was reaching down, almost falling out of the helicopter. The pilot tried to pull them all up, and Duban's feet, Haldane could see, left the ground. In between them was the lifeless Aliyyah, now not holding on to the ladder, but stretched between them, swinging out into the draft, robes and hair billowing violently. He could no longer see her face. He could hear urgent talking above him, among the crew. The pilot dropped the craft down again, and Duban's feet touched the ground. The moment they did, Ma'ahaba was upon him, pulling him away from Aliyyah and Haldane and the ladder. So that now they formed a ladder themselves, a human chain hanging from the sky.

"Captain. This man's screwing up the mission. Who the hell is he?" There were more words from above which he couldn't make out, the 'copter jumped upwards again, and then the night was suddenly lit up. Haldane heard the retort of the gun a moment later.

In that instant of light he saw the first splashes of red blood. "Aliyyah!" He screamed. But now she reacted and looked up at him, her eyes alive again but full of tears and dismay. She looked at the aircraft and then at him as if she

"The pilot tried to pull them all up and Duban's feet ... left the ground.
In between them was the lifeless Aliyyah, ... robes and hair billowing ..."

had no idea what either of them were and how she was hanging perilously in mid-air.

On the ground below, Duban and Ma'ahaba lay flat. He heard Aliyyah, under the growl of the engine, call both their names. Then she leaped from the ladder, staggering onto the hard earth below. He was just about to follow when he felt the arm of his comrade on his shoulder, and the snap of a safety harness being fastened to him. He yelled "No!" and tried to loosen the catch, but couldn't.

"Let me go!"

His feet left the ladder and he swung below the slashing blades, felt himself being pulled up in jolts towards the cabin. The beam of torchlight swept to and fro over the scene below him. Aliyyah on her knees over the two still bodies. When the beam swept back again Haldane saw a bloom of crimson spread out over the clearing.

Then he saw Duban get to his knees. Aliyyah looked up at him, and he thought he saw hatred in her eyes. The soldier above was hauling him in, but Haldane resisted, spellbound by that red flower unfolding. Springing, he now understood, not from the old man, but from Ma'ahaba, her head open and broken, her body still as stone.

The Warrior Returns

His limbs and his neck were aching again, though whether from the same wounds as before, he didn't know or care. He walked along the lane he had not seen for so long, up the hill, and saw appearing at its end the house.

His vision was blurry, as was his memory. Though he knew everything that had happened, could list them in order, it all felt artificial. Only the memory of Ma'ahaba lying dead, Aliyyah's sharp eyes, and Duban waving his little fist, felt real.

The rest of the flight back to base was vague. He had been pushed into a seat by the crew and fastened down. He could still hear himself shouting, screaming, but could no longer remember his own words.

Then there had been an inquiry, then the summary hearing. There were warrant officers, advisers, his own testimony, accusations made against him, the beginning of the court martial – all of it muffled sounds and images in his head, as though he had watched them on, or through, a screen. His every action had been studied, argued over, questioned, defended. From the moment of the crash... What had happened between the aircraft personnel that morning? Had Captain Thomas Haldane tried to help his fellows, Gunner Kane and Pilot Samson? How had he alone managed to walk free? Who had helped him and why? To all of these queries he tried to answer as simply and as honestly as he could, though his answers had sounded improbable even to him.

More and more questions. An infinity of them. How had he managed to salvage the radio? Wasn't it

"He walked along the lane he had not seen for so long, up the hill,
and saw appearing at its end the house."

surprising that, while a craft as robust as the Wildcat had all but been obliterated, a simple radio had survived intact? And who had taught him to operate it? Whilst he was MIA, to whom had he spoken and what had he told them?

Between all the questions there were different places. First his own quarters and bunk, then a cell. Then a flight and a different cell, courtrooms. Had he briefed the rescue party correctly? His unit had expected more men, perhaps compromised allied fighters, perhaps prisoners of war. Instead, so far as they could ascertain, there were only two women and an elderly man. What was behind the scuffle that had impaired the rescue operation? Had Captain Haldane endangered the rescue mission and the crew's lives by exposing them to an ill-prepared plan and enemy agents? Who had given the order to fire?

Every morning and every night, before and after interrogations, he had pleaded for news. Could he speak to Aliyyah, the younger woman? The radio was still at the house – they could make contact. Was Ma'ahaba dead? All requests were refused, no information was given him. He was stripped of his post, dismissed. He had had a duty of care, had not followed procedures, had acted improperly in action. Thomas Haldane was cast out. Sent back to the world, dishonoured.

And now he was walking, in a suit he had not worn for years that hung loosely round his shoulders and frayed at his heels. The hill up to the house seemed steeper and longer than he remembered it. And he felt so alone, under the weight of his longing, and his dread.

Yet in his loneliness he felt them around him. The old man, the beautiful girl and, especially, Ma'ahaba. He thought he could hear them whispering to him.

"The patient seldom understands the ways of the physician, my friend."

Aliyyah singing gaily: "Love awaits you! Love's not

grown in the garden, or sold in the bazaar. King or serv-ant, the price is your head. O miser, a cheap price to pay!"

And Ma'ahaba laughing. "To get what you want, you must first learn to live with what you fear."

He had no idea how much time had passed, but still he could not piece together what had gone wrong the morn-ing of the crash. It all happened so fast. The blink of an eye. He had been told that little could be deduced from the crash site. The AgustaWestland Wildcat had been found, but in pieces, spread out over an area of more than three square miles. But of his colleagues no trace had been found. They had been awarded posthumous honours, both. But Michael Samson and Simon Kane had been obliterated. His comrades-in-arms lifted bodily from the world, launched, in infinitesimal pieces of matter, into the stars. He felt now that something of them, too, remained, in the air, drifting around him wherever he went. Mick and Si, more present, even here at his father's house, than he was himself.

Opening the gate he thought he heard in its creaking the voice of Ma'ahaba: "The glory of the fall is never to land." At the end of the driveway there was a light on in the study. The late summer trees hung heavily overhead, dripping rain on him. His father was sitting at his desk, as Haldane knew he would be. The son hung his head lower at the sight. The soldier returning home disgraced.

And yet there was still some pride left in him, a shard of defiance. He had gone and he had fought. He had been vanquished, but had learned something. The soldier was not returning empty-handed. He'd seen hell and he'd seen heaven. He was a man of the world. Perhaps he had found love, and now he knew hate. The beauty and the torment would live forever inside him. He was returning full of holes, like the victim of action, of gunfire. Holes in him, for Ma'ahaba and Duban. He was bleeding invisibly, as if half his flesh was torn away, the absence of Aliyyah draining him. And more cavities, one for every question, a hollow for each unsatisfactory answer he had given, for the loss of comrades and companions. A chasm for the final ice-green of betrayal in Aliyyah's eyes.

When he looked up again, his father was no longer at the window, alarming Haldane more than he had expected. But he returned a moment later, helping the soldier's mother to the window. She still did not look old which made her sickness all the more cruel. But she seemed to see him. Perhaps she even knew, somewhere deep inside, who this bedraggled young man was. In her eyes was that glow, as if she saw the world differently, perceived what Haldane could not. But still she stared a notch or so above his head.

His father held her tight, and the two of them stepped close to the window pane, as though he was making sure his sight wasn't deceiving him. His ageing face full of wonder. Haldane struggled up the last rise in the hill and saw dad open his arms to him, and hoped it was a gesture of joy, not in the son's defeat, but in his return.

Acknowledgements

Bewitch us to death
with gods and beasties,
tall wifies' old lore.
Fairy tails.
Makie-uppie places, greater than this.

Thank you, Robert Louis Stevenson, for "Olalla". And for "Isle of Voices". The story of "Olalla" has intrigued me since I read it as a teenager, and is the inspiration for Aliyyah.

Jekyll and Hyde is in here too and lots more of Tusitala's yarns. Books and stories come out of the books and stories we've read and heard. In this case there are too many to mention. *One Thousand and One Nights* has been a passion for almost as long as Stevenson. Stories to keep the morning at bay, hold back the terrors of the night. Marina Warner's work on Arabian Nights and fairy tales helped me hugely.

Thanks to Anthony Grayling's *The Good Book*, itself a compendium of thousands of books that preceded it. And holy books – the Bible, Qur'an, Tanakh, the sutras and the Tibetan Book of the Dead. I'm not claiming to have read them all cover to cover, but have dipped into them all over the years. Duban would say that my eye was directed, but in truth every now and then something simply chimed with me and made its way, in one form or another, into this wee creation here.

Thanks too to other writers, particularly Scottish ones, Spanish-language ones, and in this case those from Jewish and Islamic traditions. Lorca and Di Mambro, Rumi and Márquez, Dylan and Saadi and Cohen.

More particularly still, those I've talked with and who gave me ideas, often without their knowing it. For one, Allan Cameron – also my publisher, editor and friend. In praise of the garrulous indeed! He is that kind of magpie writer and thinker, forever finding shiny facts and fictions and sharpened stanzas, and seeing the connections between them. Rosemary Goring for years of talking books. Paul Cuddihy for encouragement and wit and songs. J. David Simons for opening up a new dimension in the writing of this. There will be others. Lots. Perhaps you'll spot them. Words and thoughts and ideas I've read and heard and discussed and that have stayed with me, nagged at me.

And thanks to friends. Liam and Eddie, and all that magic talking in Spanish bars and restaurants after long days cycling up hills. Thanks to Fergal who, if he isn't already, should be keeping a tally of my thefts.

And my best friend of all – we share books, thoughts, and now a long history together. All my books are as much yours, Moira, as mine. And to my family, those who went before, follow on, and those with whom I walk in step. As Ma'ahaba says, stories and dreams – we need to do *something* with them.

> *My Scotland exists in the minds of others,*
> *a long night's journey*
> *through impossible passes*
> *to panoramas of dreams and perhapses.*